MW00918502

Mindy Kim,
Class President

Don't miss more fun adventures
with **Mindy Kim**!

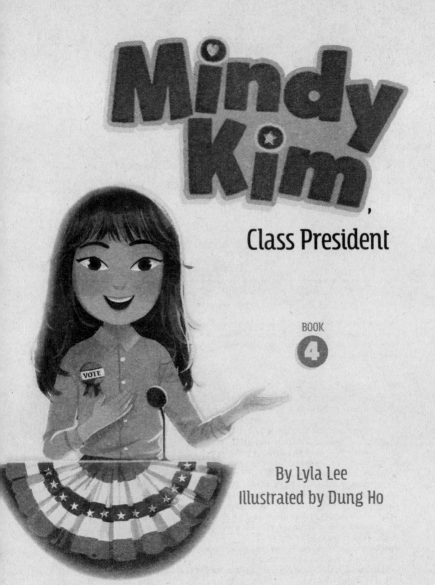

Mindy Kim,

Class President

BOOK
4

By Lyla Lee
Illustrated by Dung Ho

ALADDIN
New York London Toronto Sydney New Delhi

If you purchased this book without a cover, you should be aware that this book is stolen property. It was reported as "unsold and destroyed" to the publisher, and neither the author nor the publisher has received any payment for this "stripped book."

This book is a work of fiction. Any references to historical events, real people, or real places are used fictitiously. Other names, characters, places, and events are products of the author's imagination, and any resemblance to actual events or places or persons, living or dead, is entirely coincidental.

🦅 ALADDIN
An imprint of Simon & Schuster Children's Publishing Division
1230 Avenue of the Americas, New York, New York 10020
First Aladdin paperback edition September 2020
Text copyright © 2020 by Lyla Lee
Illustrations copyright © 2020 by Dung Ho
Also available in an Aladdin hardcover edition.
All rights reserved, including the right of reproduction in whole or in part in any form.
ALADDIN and related logo are registered trademarks of Simon & Schuster, Inc.
For information about special discounts for bulk purchases, please contact Simon & Schuster Special Sales at 1-866-506-1949 or business@simonandschuster.com.
The Simon & Schuster Speakers Bureau can bring authors to your live event. For more information or to book an event contact the Simon & Schuster Speakers Bureau at 1-866-248-3049 or visit our website at www.simonspeakers.com.
Designed by Laura Lyn DiSiena
The illustrations for this book were rendered digitally.
The text of this book was set in Haboro.
Manufactured in the United States of America 0820 OFF
2 4 6 8 10 9 7 5 3 1
Library of Congress Control Number 2020934962
ISBN 978-1-5344-4017-3 (hc)
ISBN 978-1-5344-4016-6 (pbk)
ISBN 978-1-5344-4018-0 (eBook)

To all the girls out there who
want to be president one day.
You can do it!

Chapter 1

My name is Mindy Kim. I am eight years old, and I'm now in third grade!

So far, third grade isn't as easy as second grade. There is a lot more homework, and the math is harder. But there are lots of fun new things too! We have new responsibilities, like helping our teacher, Mr. Brady, around the classroom. We also have a classroom guinea pig, Mr. Snuffles!

I sit next to Mr. Snuffles in class. He's a little smelly, but he's so cute that I don't mind. Mr. Snuffles has brown-and-white fur and large black eyes. Occasionally, he makes funny little squeaking sounds that make me smile. On special occasions, like someone's birthday, Mr. Brady puts a bow tie around his neck!

Today Mr. Brady announced that we're having class-president elections.

"I know it's October, and everyone's probably busy preparing for Halloween this weekend, but it's been two weeks since our old class president, Dill, moved away," he explained. "So we need someone to replace him. And what could be a better time to have a class election than next week, when the adults in our country will vote for a new president of the United States?"

Dill was really nice, and he was such a good class president, too! He was one of the first friends I made when I moved to Florida last year. I was really sad when he moved away.

Priscilla raised her hand. She's the girl who sits at the front of the class and always asks questions.

"Yes, Priscilla?"

"What do we have to do during the class-president election?" she asked.

"Oh, I think you were absent when we had the election last time," said Mr. Brady. "Why don't we go through the rules one more time? It's always good for everyone to have a reminder."

He smiled at all of us. "Anyone who wants to run for class president has to give a speech about why they should win. You will also need to make campaign posters and bring them to class by this Friday. You should memorize the speech if you can, so be sure to ask your mom or dad for help!"

Mr. Snuffles squeaked, as if agreeing with Mr. Brady. I wondered who Mr. Snuffles would vote for if he could!

Mr. Brady continued. "Next Monday you will give your speech, and then everyone in the class will vote for our new president. I'll pass out a fill-in-the-blank speech-planning sheet to help everyone out!"

He started handing out the sheets. When he gave me one, I stared at the paper.

We had to talk about so many different things, like our three best traits and what we would do as class president. It looked fun, but it also made me really nervous. I tucked the paper away in my backpack because just reading it made me feel scared.

When we'd first had classroom elections in August, I'd been too scared to run. I like people, but I don't like speaking in front of the class. Whenever we have to present in front of everybody for special projects, it makes my tummy hurt and I feel really dizzy.

"You should run this time, Mindy!" said Sally, my best friend. "You have so many friends. You'll win for sure!"

I shook my head. "I don't know . . . speeches are scary."

"Well, you can practice! My mom said she used to hate speeches too, but it's easy for her now since she does it almost every day for her job. You just need to practice lots and you'll be okay!"

Sally's belief in me made me all warm and fuzzy inside. Maybe she was right. Maybe I could really be the next class president!

But I was still scared. What if I froze and couldn't

remember a single thing? What if I talked too fast or too slow? What if my voice sounded funny and made everyone laugh?

I needed to talk to Dad. He would help me figure out what to do!

Chapter 2

Later that day, when it was time for dinner, I went into the kitchen to help Dad reheat leftovers. Yesterday Dad had made japchae, yummy Korean noodles with meat and vegetables, so we were eating that today, too.

Dad and I were both really hungry, so we watched the plate of food go around and around in the microwave. Theodore, my dog, also came over to watch!

"Dad?" I asked while we were waiting.

I opened my mouth to tell Dad about the class-president elections. But when I did, nothing came out! It was like I couldn't talk all of a sudden.

Just thinking about running for class president made my stomach feel all funny inside!

"Yes, Mindy?" Dad asked. He looked worried when I didn't say anything.

At that moment, the microwave bell went off.

"Dinner is ready!" I yelled really loudly.

Dad winced. "I can see that, Mindy. Is everything okay?"

"Yup! Totally fine. Nothing to see here! Of course!"

Dad stared at me as he put the japchae onto separate plates for the two of us. He didn't say a single thing. He just raised *one* eyebrow.

I sighed. Dad always knows what to do to get me talking.

"We're having a class-president election next week!" I blurted out. "Dill was our president, but he moved away, so we need a new one."

"Oh, that's very cool! Are you thinking of running?" Dad asked.

I hung my head and didn't say anything as I followed him to the table.

"I don't know," I said as I sat down. "I want to!

But we have to make a speech. And I hate talking in front of other people."

Dad set the plates of japchae down at the table and smiled at me.

"Well, this sounds like an excellent learning opportunity, Mindy! Best-case scenario, you'll become class president. Worst-case scenario, this will be a good chance to practice speaking in front of others. I think you should definitely try running. You'd make a great president!"

My heart beat really fast.

"Do you really think so, Appa?" I asked, calling him the Korean word for "Daddy."

"Yup! Let me know if you need my help with your speech. I'm more than happy to help out."

Dad and I started eating our food. The japchae was good, as usual, but I couldn't really focus on eating it. I was too busy thinking about my speech. Even with the guidelines Mr. Brady had given us, I had no idea what to write.

Theodore sat at my feet and looked up at me like he always does when I eat.

He was really cute, but I tried my best to ignore him. Dad says I shouldn't give him any food from the table, or else it'll become a bad habit. I went back to thinking about my speech.

"Dad, can you help me with my speech after dinner?" I asked. "Mr. Brady gave us a sheet to help us plan it out."

Dad beamed. "Of course, Mindy! We can work on it together after dinner."

After we ate dinner and washed the dishes, Dad and I sat together at the dining room table to work on the speech.

"Hmm, so, it looks like the easiest part is the beginning. All you have to do is say your name and how old you are."

"That's easy-peasy!" I said. On the piece of paper, I wrote *Mindy* in the first blank and *eight* in the second.

"Next you have to write the three things that are most important to you."

This was really easy too. "You, Theodore, and my friends!"

Dad smiled. "Good! Next you need to write three of your best traits. A trait is a word that people can use to describe you."

I thought long and hard. "Well, you always say I'm responsible. And Sally says I'm funny. But I can't think of a last one!"

"Hmm, well, you try your best to help me and your friends, so I think you're also really caring!"

I beamed. "Thanks, Dad!"

It was now time for the hardest part. At the end of our speech, we were supposed to talk about how we would help the class and why everyone should vote for us.

I gripped my pencil tightly. There were so many things I wanted to say, but there were only three blanks. I couldn't choose!

"Hmm," said Dad when I hadn't written anything for a while. "What platform do you want to run on, Mindy?"

"A platform?" I asked. "What's that?"

"A platform is like the mission for your campaign. What are some of the things you're going to

focus on and change as the class president?"

I stared down at my paper again. But no matter how hard I thought, I couldn't choose what to say.

"How about you think on it a bit more?" Dad said after a while. "I'm sure you'll think of something soon, and today's only Tuesday, so you have plenty of time. I'd be happy to look over it again when you're done!"

"Okay," I said. "Thanks, Appa!"

Even though I had no idea how to finish my speech, I still felt a lot better about everything. Writing the speech wasn't so scary with Dad's help!

Chapter 3

After thinking long and hard about my platform, I chose three things: friends, kindness, and snacks. I wanted to be everyone's friend, be nice to everyone, and give them really yummy snacks. Friendship and food are both really important parts of my life!

The next day at school, I showed my speech-planning sheet to Mr. Brady and told him I was running for class president.

"Excellent!" Mr. Brady said. "Looking forward to hearing your speech next Monday, Mindy! Remember to have the posters ready by this Friday. Oh, and wear this sticker on Monday. It's so that people know you're running for class president."

He gave me a red-white-and-blue sticker with the word VOTE! on it.

"Can I also bring snacks on Monday?" I asked. "Snacks are a really important part of my campaign!"

"Sure!" replied Mr. Brady. "Everyone can bring snacks, stickers . . . whatever you want to promote your campaign. Just be sure that your dad e-mails me ahead of time to tell me what you're bringing, in case anyone has allergies."

"Okay!"

When I showed my speech to Sally during lunch, she smiled.

"I really like your platform. Friendship, kindness, and snacks. That's so you!"

When I first moved to Florida last year, I tried to make new friends by trading my seaweed snacks with everybody at lunch. That's how I became friends with Sally!

"Thanks!" I said. "Are you running for class president?"

Sally shook her head. "Nope. But you have my vote!"

"Hey, that's not fair!" said Brandon, a boy who sits at our lunch table. "You haven't even heard her speech yet, and you're already voting for her?"

"Yeah, of course!" Sally replied. "She's my friend!"

Brandon isn't really our friend, but he still sits with us at lunch because our table is where his friends like to sit. He, Sally, and I had a big fight last year over my yummy seaweed-snack business. He's one of the meanest kids at our school.

"Are you running too, Brandon?" I asked. Mr. Brady hadn't announced who else was running, so I had no idea who I was up against.

"Yeah," Brandon said with a big, ugly grin. "That means we're rivals. I can't wait to beat you!"

"As if!" Sally exclaimed. "Mindy is way nicer than you. She's going to win!"

"We'll see about that," replied Brandon.

Suddenly I remembered what people said in movies when they were competing against each other.

I stuck my hand out. I didn't want to shake hands

with Brandon, but I had to be nice to him since I was promising to be everyone's friend as part of my platform.

"Let the best kid win," I said.

Brandon laughed and shook my hand.

"Sure. But don't cry when I beat you!"

The bell rang, and Brandon ran away, laughing.

"Jerk!" Sally called after him.

"It's okay," I said, clenching my fists in determination. "I'm going to beat him for sure."

Even though I was still scared about the speech, I wanted to win the election even more now that I knew Brandon was running too.

I couldn't let a mean kid like him become class president! Even if that meant I had to face my fears and be brave.

Chapter 4

Eunice, my babysitter, picked me up after school. Dad was working late today, so I had to stay at her house until he came back.

"Hey, how was your day, Mindy?" Eunice asked when I got into her car. "Are you excited for Halloween?"

"Yeah!" I exclaimed. "I'm also running for class president next week, so it's going to be really busy!"

It was easier to say out loud now that I was officially running. Plus, I had a really important reason to win now!

"Oh, how cool!" said Eunice. "Do you guys have

to give a speech? That's what we had to do when I was in elementary school."

"Yeah . . . ," I said. "That's the hardest part. We also have to make posters."

I looked down at my feet. Even though I wanted to win, I was still scared about the speech.

"Aw, it's okay, Mindy. I'll help you practice! How about we work on posters and go through your speech after we finish our homework? Oliver and I can be your audience."

Oliver the Maltese is Eunice's dog. He is fluffy and really cute! Theodore is the cutest dog in my book, but Oliver comes really close. Eunice and Oliver are both really nice, so practicing the speech in front of them didn't sound too scary.

"Okay!" I said.

On our way to Eunice's house, we stopped at Walmart to get supplies for posters. We bought poster paper in lots of different colors, including pink, green, white, and orange!

"I have markers and other supplies at home, so we can just use those," Eunice said.

"Wow, thanks, Unni! You're the best."

Unni is the Korean word for "older sister." Eunice isn't really my sister, but in Korean culture, I still have to call her that out of respect because she's older than me.

"No problem. Glad I can help!"

When we arrived at Eunice's house, Mrs. Park, Eunice's mom, greeted us at the door. Oliver the Maltese peeked his head out too!

"Hi, Mindy!" Mrs. Park said.

Oliver barked and wagged his tail in a really friendly way. I petted him on the head because he was a very good boy.

"Mindy has to make posters and give a speech for school," Eunice said. "She's running for class president!"

"How exciting!" replied Mrs. Park. "I still remember when you ran for class president, Eunice. You were so cute! Mindy, let me know if I can help."

"I sure will!" I said. Everyone in Eunice's family is so nice!

Homework was pretty hard. Math is my least

favorite class. Today I had a worksheet full of word problems about counting money. Word problems are really confusing, and I didn't know what some of them meant, but Eunice helped me when I got stuck.

When I finished my homework, Eunice called me out to the living room. She had the poster paper spread out on the floor.

"All right, Mindy," she said. "How about you tell me what to write and I'll help you by neatly writing your slogans on the posters? We can decorate the posters together later."

"Okay!"

We sat on the floor to make the posters. After some thinking, I came up with lots of fun slogans:

You've Got a Friend in Mindy Kim!

Vote Mindy, Vote Snacks!

Vote Mindy Kim, Everyone's Friend!

"Wow, all of these are great!" Eunice said once she was done writing them. "Now do you want to decorate them?"

"Yeah!"

I tried making the posters as cute as I could. I

drew stick figures, stars, and even flowers!

When we were done, Eunice gave me a high five. "Way to go, Mindy! These look really cute!"

"Hooray!" I cheered.

But now that we were done with the posters, it was time for the hardest part. I had to practice my speech!

Eunice helped me put the posters in a safe place and then sat on the living room couch with Oliver on her lap. Mrs. Park came over to sit on the couch too.

Everyone was staring at me!

"Okay, Mindy," Eunice said, "we're ready for you. Tell us your speech!"

My face felt really hot, like I had a fever. I was holding the speech-planning sheet, but my hands were shaking so much that I couldn't read what it said.

"H-hi," I said. My voice came out really small and quiet, like a mouse's! "My n-name is Mindy Kim."

Eunice gave me a big smile. "Maybe speak a little bit louder, Mindy!"

I glanced over at Mrs. Park and Oliver. Oliver wagged his tail at me, and Eunice's mom gave me a supportive grin.

"H-hi!" I said, trying my best to be louder. "My name is M-Mindy! I am eight years old. I . . . I . . ."

I wanted to cry. This was too scary!

"It's okay, Mindy, just try again!" Eunice said.

Oliver the Maltese wagged his tail, but even that wasn't enough for me to keep going.

I hung my head and stared at the floor. "I can't. It's too scary."

"That's all right," said Eunice. "A lot of people are bad at giving speeches. In fact, I'm pretty sure most people are at first, including me! You just have to practice, okay?"

"Okay," I said with a sigh. I was really disappointed in myself. How was I going to say the speech in front of the entire class?

"Maybe you should try saying the speech to stuffed animals first," Eunice suggested. "That's how I always practice my speeches."

"Stuffed animals?"

"Yeah!" Eunice laughed. "I still have all of mine. Even some grown-ups still have them, and that's perfectly okay! Anyway, what I like to do is put all the stuffed animals on my bed and say my speech to them. It really helps because I can make as many mistakes as I want and they'll still listen politely! Why don't you try doing that too?"

"Okay," I said.

I wasn't sure if it was going to work, but I was willing to try anything to get better at making a speech!

Chapter 5

That night, I put all my stuffed animals on my bed like Eunice suggested. A lot of them were dusty from being under the bed for so long, but I gave them all a good shake.

"Sorry, friends," I said. "Hope it wasn't too scary down there."

I put Mr. Shiba front and center, along with Mr. Toe Beans. And then I put Mrs. Poodle, Mr. Koala, and Ms. Alligator in the next row. Soon I had a whole audience waiting for my speech!

"Okay," I said. "Please be nice to me. This is my first speech!"

The stuffed animals didn't say anything, but they

still looked nice. Eunice was right. They were really polite!

I stared down at my speech-planning sheet. My hands weren't shaking like they were in Eunice's house, but my tummy still felt kind of funny.

"H-hi," I said.

I looked up from my paper. The stuffed animals were still staring at me, but they weren't scary at all. They were actually really cute!

I breathed out and tried again.

"Hi! My name is Mindy Kim. I am eight years old."

I looked up. The stuffed animals stared back. I smiled.

"I am running for class president! The things that are most important to me are my friends and my family."

Eunice was right. Practicing my speech was a lot easier with the help of my stuffed animal friends!

In no time at all, I finished my speech. It wasn't easy, but I still did it!

I tried giving my speech again. This time I was a bit better!

I was about to recite my speech a third time when Theodore came into my room. He jumped on my bed and grabbed Ms. Alligator!

"Theodore, no!"

Luckily, Theodore's legs are pretty short, so I caught him before he could run off with Ms. Alligator.

"Bad dog," I said. "Ms. Alligator isn't your toy. Give her back!"

He dropped Ms. Alligator and licked my face, so I couldn't stay mad long!

I giggled. "You're lucky you're cute."

I scooped Theodore up into a big hug.

While I was hugging Theodore, Dad popped his head into my bedroom.

"Hey, Mindy, how's that speech going? I heard you practicing. Do you feel ready to say it in front of me now?"

I gulped. Suddenly I was scared again.

"Not yet," I said. "I need to practice some more!"

"Well, all right. Just let me know, okay? I'm more than happy to listen to your speech whenever you're ready."

"Okay," I said.

Dad looked at Theodore, who was still in my arms. "Hmm, is he being distracting? Here, let me try something."

He went downstairs and came back with a brand-new bone.

"Here," he said, giving the bone to Theodore. "Hopefully, he'll be less trouble while he's chewing the bone."

I put Theodore on the floor. "Now, you be a good boy so I can practice my speech!"

Right away, Theodore sat on the floor and started chewing on the bone.

CRUNCH-CRUNCH-CRUNCH.

He looked so happy!

"Good idea, Dad!" I said. "Thanks!"

"You're welcome. Good luck with your speech!"

Dad left my room. As he was chewing the bone, Theodore stared up at me from the floor like he was one of my stuffed animals. He was now part of my audience!

I picked up my speech-planning sheet again. I

could hear the loud crunching sounds of Theodore gnawing on his bone, but the sound was so funny that it helped me feel less nervous.

"Hi, my name is Mindy Kim," I said. "I am running for class president!"

CRUNCH-CRUNCH-CRUNCH.

I laughed. Practicing my speech had just become way more fun!

Chapter 6

The next day after school, Eunice picked me up again.

"How's the speech going?" she asked when I got into her car.

"Pretty good!" I said. "Your idea worked, and I practiced a lot."

"That's great! Do you have to memorize the speech too?"

"We don't have to, but Mr. Brady said we should if we can."

Eunice sat up straighter in her seat. "You should! It looks a lot more professional if you do. It'll help you be less nervous, too! I always memorized my speeches, even when I was a little kid."

I gulped. Practicing the speech was hard enough—I didn't think I could memorize it too.

"If you're sure . . . ," I said.

"Don't worry, Mindy," Eunice replied. "You can practice with me and Oliver again!"

I still didn't know if I could do it, but I remembered what I thought about having to be brave. I had no idea if Brandon would memorize his speech, but it'd look really bad if he did and I didn't.

"Okay," I said. "Let's do it!"

Back at Eunice's house, I stood in the middle of Eunice's room while Eunice and Oliver the Maltese lay on her bed. Eunice held my speech-planning sheet in front of her as I tried to memorize it.

"Hi, my name is Mindy. I am eight years old and I am running for class president," I said. "The things . . ."

I trailed off. Giving the speech wasn't so scary anymore, but I couldn't remember what I'd said next!

"'The things that are the most important to me are . . . ,'" read Eunice.

"Right!" I said. "The things that are the most important to me are my friends and my family. I live with my dad and my dog, Theodore the Mutt! I am . . ."

I stopped again. Memorizing was really hard!

"Remember, Mindy," Eunice said. "The speech has three parts: telling the class about yourself, talking about what's important to you, and, finally, saying what you'd do to make the class better. You don't have to say what you wrote word for word, but just try to do those three things!"

I nodded and kept going.

"I am confident and love my friends. Being everybody's friend and helping others is really important to me!"

Eunice smiled. "You almost got it! I think you just need to practice a bit more and you'll be all set."

At that moment, Mrs. Park came into Eunice's room with a tray full of cookies shaped like jack-o'-lanterns.

"Happy almost Halloween!" she said. "I know

Halloween isn't until Saturday, but I wanted to make some cookies now so that you girls could bring them to school tomorrow."

"Wow, thanks, Mom!" said Eunice. She looked at me. "You've been working so hard, Mindy. You deserve a cookie break!"

"Yay!" I cheered.

"Come downstairs to eat so you don't get crumbs on the carpet," Mrs. Park said. "I also made ghost-shaped cookies!"

Eunice and I did what she said. While we were eating the cookies in the kitchen, Eunice asked me, "Do you know what you're dressing up as for Halloween yet?"

"Yup! Halloween is my favorite holiday, so Dad and I always prepare super early. We already got our costumes a few weeks ago."

Eunice laughed. "That's so cute! What are you going as?"

"A vet! That's what I want to be when I grow up. How about you?"

Eunice shook her head. "I'm too busy to go

trick-or-treating this year. I have a big exam coming up next week, so I'm just staying in and studying!"

I gasped. I felt so bad for Eunice! I'd be so sad if I couldn't celebrate Halloween.

Eunice smiled at my reaction. "It's okay. I'll hand out candy, so I still get to see fun costumes. Be sure to have *all* the fun for both you and me!"

I nodded very seriously. I was now determined to have the best Halloween ever!

Chapter 7

On Friday, the night before Halloween, I finally felt brave enough to practice my speech in front of Dad.

When I came out of my room, Dad was watching TV on the couch with Theodore. They were watching a fun action movie, but Dad turned off the TV when he saw me. I could tell he wanted to give me his full attention.

"Ready?" he asked.

I nodded. I'd said my speech so many times to my stuffed animal friends that I'd memorized everything! I hoped I would be able to say it to Dad, too.

I stood in front of the TV and let out a big breath.

Dad gave me a nice, encouraging smile.

And then . . . I gave my speech! It was still pretty scary, and I had to start over three times, but on my third try I made it all the way through.

By that time Theodore was fast asleep on Dad's lap. He was so adorable that I didn't mind.

When I finished, Dad got up to clap. Theodore fell out of his lap and yelped.

"Oh no!" I yelled. "Theodore, are you okay?"

Theodore got back on his feet and wagged his tail. Dad and I laughed.

"Silly dog," I said.

I gave Theodore a belly rub. Dad came over and started scratching Theodore's head. The dog stuck out his tongue, looking really happy. He is so spoiled!

"You improved so much, Mindy!" Dad said. "I think you'll just have to practice a bit more and then you'll be all set!"

I beamed. "You really think so?"

"Yup! Keep working at it. Regardless of whether or not you get elected on Monday, I'm so proud of you for all the work you're putting into this."

"Thanks, Appa," I said.

"Hey, why don't we watch a fun movie, since tomorrow is Halloween?" Dad suggested. "I bet you could use a break."

I gasped. "Can we watch a scary movie?"

Last year Dad had said I was too young for scary movies. But I was eight now! That meant I was old enough, right?

Dad laughed nervously. "Hmm, maybe we can watch a scary movie for kids! How about *Halloweentown*?"

"Okay!"

I'd heard some kids talking about *Halloween-town* in school, but I'd never watched it myself. I was really excited!

Dad made some popcorn, and I plopped down on the couch in between Dad and Theodore. It was the perfect start to Halloween!

Chapter 8

The next morning, I jumped out of bed, all excited. It was Halloween, my favorite holiday!

"Happy Halloween!" I yelled.

Theodore barked and jumped out of bed after me. He looked really surprised.

"Sorry, boy," I said, petting him on the head. "I didn't mean to scare you!"

I changed into my vet costume, which was a doctor's white coat over pink, paw print-patterned pants. It also came with a stethoscope, and I picked up Mr. Shiba and put him under my arm as a finishing touch. I was ready for Halloween!

I went downstairs with Theodore. Dad was waiting for us in a pirate costume!

"Arr!" he said. "Shiver me theaters!"

I giggled. "It's 'timbers,' Appa."

Dad smiled. "I know. I just wanted to make you laugh!"

While we were eating breakfast, Dad checked the route to the fall carnival on his phone.

In honor of Halloween, our town was holding a big carnival, with a haunted house, a pumpkin patch, and fun rides! I was most looking forward to the haunted house, because I like scary things. I really hoped Dad would let me go into it.

We picked up Julie, Dad's girlfriend, on our way to the fall carnival. She was wearing a witch costume, and she even had a broom and a black-cat doll! She saw that I was carrying Mr. Shiba and gave me a high five.

"Great costume, Mindy! I like your dog," she said.

"Thanks! I like your cat!"

At the carnival we met up with Sally's family, the Johnsons. Sally has a big family, with two sisters and two parents! They were all dressed as super-heroes, which I thought was super cool!

Sally was dressed up as Wonder Woman. Her mom was Batgirl, and her dad was Batman! Mrs. Johnson had squarish blue glasses and looked like a grown-up version of Sally. Mr. Johnson had red hair and a nice smile. Both of Sally's parents looked really friendly. I've met Sally's mom before, but this was the first time I'd seen her dad.

Sally's parents shook hands with Dad and Julie while Sally introduced me to her sisters.

Sally pointed at her oldest sister, who was wearing a Catwoman costume.

"That's Martha. She's in ninth grade."

Martha smiled at me. She has braces, which make her look really cool. She has red hair, like Mr. Johnson.

"Hi!" I said. "Do you know Eunice? She's my babysitter, and she's in high school too!"

Martha shook her head. "There are a *lot* of Eunices at my school, but I probably don't know her. It's a big school!"

"And this is Patricia," Sally said, pointing at her other sister. "She's in sixth grade."

Patricia was dressed as Supergirl! She has blond hair like Sally.

"Hi, how's middle school?" I asked Patricia. I always heard about high school from Eunice, but I'd never really heard about middle school. It was where I was going after elementary school, so I was pretty curious.

"It's okay." Patricia shrugged. "Elementary school was more fun, though."

Once we were all done saying hi, Dad asked, "So, girls, what do you want to do first?"

"The haunted house!" I yelled, and at the same time Sally and her sisters said, "Pumpkin patch!"

Dad's face became a little green when he heard me say "haunted house." He doesn't like scary things like I do.

"Okay, we can definitely do everything at some point," he said. "But let's go to the pumpkin patch for now!"

I really wanted to go to the haunted house, but that was fine by me. The pumpkin patch was so cute! There were countless pumpkins in all sorts of shapes and sizes. Some of them were orange, while others were yellow and green. Some of them were normal pumpkins, while others were jack-o'-lanterns carved into various shapes. My favorite was the one carved to look like Snoopy!

After we were done exploring, we all gathered around for a group photo. I was so happy!

While we were walking out of the pumpkin patch, I heard people screaming in the haunted house.

"Dad!" I said. "Can we go to the haunted house now?"

Dad looked at me, and then at our group. "Hmm, I don't know. Mindy, you should ask if everyone else wants to go to the haunted house too."

"Sure, I'll go," said Martha. "I'm not scared."

"I–I'll pass," Patricia said. "I hate haunted houses."

"I want to go too!" yelled Sally. "But only if Mommy goes with me."

"Of course I'll go with you, sweetheart," Mrs. Johnson said. "I don't think you can go in without an adult anyway."

Dad sighed. "And I'll go with you, Mindy."

"Are you sure, Brian?" Julie asked. She looked a little worried about Dad. "I can go in with her if you want."

"Yeah, you don't have to if you don't want to, Dad," I said. "Mrs. Johnson will be there with me too!"

Dad shook his head. He looked really determined.

"No, it's okay," said Dad. "I'll do anything for you, Mindy. Even go into the haunted house. Let's go!"

"Yay!" I said. "Thanks, Dad!"

I was so excited to go to the haunted house!

Chapter 9

The haunted house was a big, scary-looking mansion. The sign at the front of the house said that it was an old house that used to be owned by a rich family a long, long time ago. Something bad had happened in the house, and now the house was haunted!

At the door there was a man dressed like a zombie and a lady dressed like an evil clown.

"Hi!" I said. "Can we go into the haunted house?"

The zombie and the clown stared down at Sally and me.

"Sure, kid," the zombie man said. "But only if your parents come with you."

"No problem! Come on, Dad!"

"O-okay, honey." Dad's voice sounded all weird and squeaky. I held his hand tight.

"It's okay, Dad," I said. "I'll protect you!"

Clown Lady laughed. "What a brave girl!" she said as she gave us all flashlights. "Have fun!"

We walked into the house. Sally and Martha stuck close to Mrs. Johnson, while I held Dad's hand. I wanted to keep him safe!

Inside the house it was really dark. We couldn't see anything aside from the light of our flashlights. There were strange sounds like a dripping faucet and someone laughing from very far away. Footsteps came from behind us.

"Boo!"

A werewolf popped out of nowhere, growling and snarling!

"Ahhh!" Dad screamed. So did Sally.

"It's okay!" Mrs. Johnson said to Sally. "There's nothing to be scared of!"

I held Dad's hand tightly and yelled at the werewolf, "I'm not afraid of you! You look like my dog, Theodore the Mutt! Go away!"

Werewolf Man looked sad as he walked away. I felt a little bad for hurting his feelings.

"Follow me," I said to our group.

As we turned the corner, a witch popped out and started cackling.

Dad and Sally screamed again, but I waved my flashlight at the witch. "Go away!"

The witch howled and ran away.

"See?" I said. "Haunted houses aren't so scary."

Mrs. Johnson laughed. "Mindy, you're one hilarious kid! Are you even shaking?"

"Nope," replied Dad. "She isn't. I'm shaking enough for the two of us."

We all laughed. Dad was so funny.

"Run away!" yelled a high-pitched voice.

A white-faced ghost snuck up on Dad and waved her arms. Dad yelped and jumped away.

"Appa, it's okay, I'll save you!"

I shined my flashlight on the ghost's face. She wailed and ran away.

"I'm so glad you're here, Mindy," Sally said. "You're braver than all of us!"

The rest of the haunted house was pretty scary, but we all made it to the exit in one piece. By the end Dad was clinging on to me very tightly. I gave him a big hug.

"It's okay, Appa. We're done!"

The workers at the exit laughed and congratulated us as we came out of the house. One of them was the werewolf from the beginning of the haunted house.

"You have a really brave daughter!" he said to Dad.

"Sorry I yelled at you, Mr. Werewolf," I said. "I was just trying to protect my dad."

The werewolf gave me a toothy grin. "It happens every time, kid–don't worry about it."

He gave me a pat on the back and handed Sally, Martha, and me ghost-shaped stickers that said I SURVIVED THE HAUNTED HOUSE!

"Yay!" I said. "I love stickers!" This was a really fun Halloween!

We met up with everyone else at the line for the Ferris wheel.

"Did y'all have fun?" Mr. Johnson asked.

"Yup!" Sally said. "Mindy protected us from everybody. She's really brave!"

"Nah, I was scared too!" I said. "But I don't think haunted houses are as scary as giving speeches."

Everyone laughed, but I was serious! I could handle witches and scary ghosts and werewolves all right, but my speech on Monday was going to be the scariest monster of them all!

Chapter 10

The day after Halloween was Sunday, the day before the class-president election. I spent all day practicing my speech and going grocery shopping with Dad. We bought snacks at the Korean supermarket so I could bring them to school on Monday.

"I checked with Mr. Brady last week, and he said no one in your class is allergic to the snacks we got today," Dad said as he tucked me into bed. "So you're all set for tomorrow!"

I pulled my blanket over my head.

"Appa, I don't think I should go to school tomorrow," I said. "My tummy feels weird."

Dad frowned and placed his hand on my

forehead. He then gave me a gentle tummy rub.

"Oh, Mindy. You're just nervous, that's all," said Dad. "It's totally okay to be scared. But just think about how brave you were at the haunted house yesterday. I'm still so amazed by what happened!"

"I just wanted to make sure you and Sally were safe," I replied. "And besides, I knew everything in the house wasn't real. Fake stuff can't hurt us. Not like real things can."

"That's true," Dad said. "Well, you were awesome at the haunted house, and I'm sure you'll be great with your speech tomorrow as well. You practiced so much!"

Thinking about my speech made the funny feeling in my belly worse. I grabbed Mr. Toe Beans, my corgi stuffed doll, and held him tightly.

"Appa, can you read me a bedtime story?"

"Sure, honey. Which story do you want me to read today?"

Dad pulled out one of my favorite books from my bookshelf. It's a collection of fun Korean folk tales that Mom and Dad bought for me the last time we visited Korea. I've already read the stories a whole bunch of times with Dad, but they're still fun!

"How about the one with the persimmon and the tiger?" I asked.

"Sure!" Dad said. He started reading me the story.

"The Tiger and the Dried Persimmon" is one of my favorite stories. It's about how a mom tricks a tiger into thinking that a dried persimmon–a yummy Korean snack–is scary, so the tiger doesn't eat her family.

"Why did the tiger think the persimmon was scary?" Even though I already knew the answer, I like how Dad always answers my question.

"Well, it's because whenever the lady mentioned the dried persimmon, her baby stopped crying. So the tiger thought that the persimmon must be *really* scary, scary enough to make babies stop crying!"

I giggled. The tiger was so silly!

Dad then read my favorite story in the entire book, "Fire Dogs." "Fire Dogs" is about the king of darkness ordering his dogs to go fetch the sun and

the moon so that the people in his kingdom can have light.

"'The sun was too hot, even for a fire dog, so the poor dogs couldn't hold on to the sun for very long,'" Dad read. "'And the moon was too cold . . . it nearly froze their mouths!' So that's the story that our ancestors told to explain why eclipses happen throughout the year. It's just the fire dogs trying to fetch!"

"Aw," I said. "I feel bad for the fire dogs. They're just trying to be good boys!"

By then I was pretty sleepy. My eyes were drooping as Dad said, "Good night, Mindy!"

He closed the door behind him, and I gave Mr. Toe Beans a big hug.

I fell asleep dreaming of tigers running away from persimmons, and fire dogs trying to grab the sun.

Chapter 11

On Monday morning I got dressed in my best presidential outfit. It was a pink button-down shirt with long black pants. I wanted to look as responsible and grown-up as I possibly could! Finally, I put the VOTE! sticker that Mr. Brady had given me on the front of my shirt. I was ready for the class-president election!

When Dad came into my room, he whistled. "Looking sharp, Mindy! Very grown-up, too."

I looked at myself in the mirror. Mom had bought the pants for me when we lived in California, and they were getting too short now. I kept growing! One of these days I'd be too big for all the clothes that Mom had bought me.

The thought made me sad, so I turned to Dad.

"I'm hungry! What's for breakfast?"

"Well, since today's a special day, I made you pancakes with chocolate chips, just the way you like them. Along with some eggs and orange juice. It's a breakfast worthy of a president for sure!"

"Hooray!" I said.

Food always makes me happy, and Dad knew just exactly what to make to cheer me up.

After breakfast, Dad drove me to school. I spotted some kids from my class who were also running for president. I could tell because they all had VOTE! stickers like I did.

Dad parked the car in the school parking lot so he could help me unload my red wagon of yummy Korean snacks. We'd bought a bunch of Choco Pie, seaweed snacks, and Pepero!

"How are you feeling about everything?" Dad asked as we went toward the school building. He pulled the wagon behind him while we walked.

"I don't know," I said. I felt better about the election than I had last week, but I still had the funny feeling in my belly.

"Well, I'll be crossing my fingers and toes for you, Mindy. Even my eyes!"

He crossed his eyes and made a silly face. I giggled. Dad is so funny.

We reached the front of the school. Dad gave me a hug before he left.

"Best of luck! Remember, no matter what happens, the most important thing is that you did your best."

"Okay, thanks, Appa."

Dad left, and I dragged my wagon of snacks through the front doors. As I went, some of my classmates turned around to point at me.

"Hey, it's the snack girl!" a kid said. His name was Peter, and he was one of Brandon's friends.

"Is she running for class president?" asked his friend Stanley.

Even though they weren't my friends, I waved hi to them on my way to Mr. Brady's class. Maybe if I was nice to them, they'd vote for me instead of Brandon!

Inside, the classroom was set up a lot differently than normal. All the desks were pushed back to make room for a podium at the front. Behind the podium were the posters of everyone running for president. All of the posters were so colorful, including mine.

The other kids also brought things like stickers, postcards, and snacks.

Sally smiled at me when she saw my wagon.

"You brought an entire wagon of snacks?" Sally asked. "That's such a great idea! Good luck! You're going to be amazing."

"Thanks, Sally! You're a good friend."

"Good morning, Mindy," said Mr. Brady. "Is that wagon of snacks for your campaign?"

"Yup!"

Mr. Brady clapped his hands together. "How creative! Please set it aside right here at the front of the classroom and go to your seat. We'll get started soon."

I did what Mr. Brady said. The first thing I saw when I sat at my seat was Mr. Snuffles. He was

wearing a red-white-and-blue bow tie. He looked so handsome!

During the morning announcements, I counted the different names on the posters. There were four other kids running besides me. One was Priscilla, the girl who always asks questions. Then there was Brandon, the mean kid. The other two were Jose and Opal, who are both really quiet and sit at the back of our class. I've only talked to Opal a few times when I've needed to borrow a piece of paper, and she is really nice!

If I didn't win, I'd be okay if anyone other than Brandon became class president.

"Okay, class," said Mr. Brady after the announcements ended. "We have five really smart and talented individuals today who want your vote for the class-president election. I'm going to need all of you to be a good audience when they're giving their speeches. Can you show them your absolute best audience behavior, just the way we practiced?"

Everyone nodded. We were all excited to hear the speeches!

"Okay, without further ado, I'll introduce you to our first candidate: Mindy Kim! Please give her a round of applause! Mindy, you're up. Step up to the podium!"

Oh no! I was first!

Everyone started clapping.

I gulped and walked around with my wagon of snacks, handing a snack to every kid before I went up to the podium.

Everyone said thanks except Brandon. He stuck his tongue out in a really mean way.

I was mad but I didn't say anything. I didn't want to make a bad impression as a presidential candidate!

When I was up at the podium, I took a deep breath and put on a brave face. I gripped both sides of the podium and set my shoulders straight, like Dad had told me to do when I was practicing.

It was time for me to give my speech!

Chapter 12

"Hi," I began. "My name is Mindy Kim, and I'm running for class president! I am eight years old."

This was always the easy part, so I said it with no problem. I looked around the classroom and saw Sally quietly cheering me on.

I nodded at her and kept going. "The things that are most important to me are my friends and my family. I live with my dad and my dog, Theodore the Mutt! I am very responsible, caring, and friendly."

Out of the corner of my eye, I saw Brandon laugh and whisper something into his friend's ear. I gulped. My legs started shaking, but I kept going.

"As class president, I would make sure to be

everyone's friend. I like giving snacks, because snacks make everyone happy. And I want to make you happy too! So I will give everyone lots of snacks and make sure that everyone knows what's happening in the classroom. I'm also going to do my best to help everybody."

I was so nervous my face was hot, and my hands were really sweaty. But I was so close to being done!

"So, vote for me, Mindy Kim! Friends, kindness, and snacks for everyone!"

I bowed, and the class clapped. I was kind of dizzy, but I felt a whole lot better now that I was done.

When I sat down in my seat, Sally patted me on the back.

"You were great!" she said. "I'd vote for you even if you weren't my friend!"

"Thanks, Sally!" I said.

"Great job, Mindy!" said Mr. Brady. "It's not easy going first, but you did an amazing job. Next up is Brandon Paulson. Brandon, come on up!"

A lot of the boys in our class cheered.

Brandon pumped up a fist into the air and said, "Yes! Finally it's my turn!"

Brandon was really good at speaking, and he didn't look nervous at all. The more he spoke, the more his friends cheered. By the time he was finished, I was sad. It looked like he was going to win for sure.

"Don't give up!" Sally said. "You never know who'll win!"

I nodded. She was right.

The other three kids were really good too. I especially liked Priscilla's speech, because she said she would help make our classroom be the very best it could ever be. Her poster had a picture of Mr. Snuffles on it, which I thought was really funny!

And then, finally, it was time to vote. Everyone wrote down their pick on a piece of paper and dropped it in the ballot box at the front of the room.

"I'll announce the winners at the end of the school day," said Mr. Brady. "But for now, it's time for lunch!"

Lunch went by super slowly, and so did the rest of the school day. I ate and worked and played at recess like I normally did, but my mind was on the class-president election. I really wanted to win!

When it was time for the class-president announcement, Mr. Brady stood at the front of the class with a small piece of paper. The paper with the name of the winner!

"Okay, class," Mr. Brady said. "Thank you for being patient. Everyone was so great. I've counted up the votes and will now announce the name of the class president. Everyone did such a good job, and I'm proud of everyone who ran. It was a close race!"

Finally it was the moment of truth!

Chapter 13

Everyone should be proud of themselves, including the people who didn't run, but voted," Mr. Brady continued. "You all made your vote count, just like your parents will hopefully do on Election Day tomorrow!"

"Just tell me I won already!" yelled Brandon.

Mr. Brady frowned. "Brandon, please calm down. Friends, what do we do when we want to talk?"

Everyone raised their hands.

"Yes, Priscilla?"

"We raise our hands!"

"Very good!"

Brandon grumbled and slumped into his seat. He was not being a good candidate!

"He's such a big baby!" said Sally. "I really hope he doesn't win."

Mr. Brady waited until we all quieted down before clearing his throat.

"Okay, class. The next president of Room 303 of Wishbone Elementary for the 2020-2021 school year is . . ."

I held my breath and crossed my fingers and toes. I closed my eyes, too. I really hoped I would win!

"Priscilla Jones!"

Everyone cheered and clapped. I opened my eyes. I was sad that I didn't win, but I was really glad that it wasn't Brandon.

"Yay, Priscilla!" I said, joining the people cheering for her. Opal and Jose said yay too. We were all happy for her!

Priscilla is always the one who asks all the questions and makes sure she understands everything. She is really smart and nice, too! I hoped she would make our class great.

The only person who wasn't cheering was Brandon. He looked really mad, and his face was red.

"No fair!" Brandon shouted. "There needs to be a recount. I deserved to win!"

"Brandon!" said Mr. Brady. "I am very disappointed in you. Please sit with me in the classroom during recess tomorrow."

I cheered on the inside. Even though I hadn't won the class-president election, I was still happy.

After school, Dad came to pick me up. Eunice usually picks me up, so I was surprised!

"I wanted to see how my presidential candidate did on her big day," Dad explained. "Luckily, I'm between projects right now, so I could leave work early! How did the election go?"

"I didn't win," I said.

"Aw, I'm so sorry, Mindy," replied Dad.

"It's okay. Priscilla Jones won, and she's really nice and smart. I'm glad she won!"

Theodore was in the car with us. He licked my face, like he wanted to cheer me up.

"Tell you what," Dad said. "Even though you didn't win, I think you still deserve a prize for working so hard on your speech. You improved so much, and that's a really big accomplishment! Why don't we go get milkshakes on our way home?"

"Yay!" I yelled.

I love milkshakes! And I love spending time with Dad.

"You know, Mindy, I was just thinking," Dad said on our way to the milkshake shop. "The things that you promised in your speech—being everyone's friend, being nice to everybody, and giving out snacks—those are all things that you can do on a day-to-day basis. You don't have to be the class president to do all three! So even though Priscilla is the class president, why don't you try to help people and set a good example for everyone else in the class too?"

"Okay, that's a great idea!"

As we sipped our mint-chocolate milkshakes, I knew Dad was right. And even though I hadn't won, I was still really happy. I'd made a really good speech! I hadn't forgotten my words! And someone really great was our class president.

Today was a good day.

Chapter 14

Priscilla is a really good president, just like I thought she'd be. She leads the class during the Pledge of Allegiance, is really fair when assigning classroom jobs, and does her best to help everyone too! Even though I'm still kind of sad that I didn't win, I'm glad that the job went to the perfect person.

A week later there was a new kid in our class. Mr. Brady said her name was Lindsey and that she'd just moved here from Minnesota. She looked really shy. She didn't know anyone and didn't have any friends yet, just like I hadn't when I was the new kid last year, in second grade.

During lunch, Lindsey sat alone. She looked really sad! I remembered what Dad had told me, and I decided to try to help.

"Hey!" I waved at her.

She pointed at herself, like she couldn't believe I was talking to her.

"Me?" she asked. Her voice sounded quiet and scared.

"Do you want to sit with me and my friend Sally?" I asked. "You can try some of my snacks!"

Lindsey's eyes widened, but then she slowly smiled.

"Okay!" she said.

Lindsey sat at our table. She didn't say anything at first. But Sally and I asked her questions to get her talking.

"What's your favorite color?" Sally wanted to know.

"And what's your favorite animal?" I asked.

"I really like blue," she said. "And I love horses! I used to have a pony at my old house. I miss her so much. Her name is Betsy!"

Lindsey showed us a picture of her pony. It was a brown pony with really cute eyes!

"Wow, you had a pony?" Sally asked. "That's so cool!"

"Sorry you don't have her anymore, though," I said.

"Oh, it's okay. She's with my grandparents now. We're going to visit them back in Minnesota on Thanksgiving!"

"That's good," I replied. "Sally and I both love dogs. I have a puppy named Theodore the Mutt!"

By the end of lunch, Sally, Lindsey, and I had talked a lot about everything and anything. We were all friends now!

Even though I hadn't won the election, I was really glad I could help Lindsey. Being the class president is important, but so is being a good friend and being kind to other people. And I was so happy that I now had a new friend!

It looked like my platform of friends, kindness, and snacks had worked after all.

Acknowledgments

First and foremost, I would like to thank *you*, Reader. Thank you for reading this book, and the previous Mindy Kim books, if you've read them. Thank you especially to those of you who've told me (either directly or through an adult) how you enjoyed reading about Mindy's adventures. The year 2020 was my first year as a published author, and it hasn't always been easy, but what makes everything worth it is hearing from readers like you. Keep reading! There are so many different worlds and stories out there. I hope you never lose your love of books.

Next, I'd like to thank my parents, who supported me when *I* ran for class president in elementary school. Thank you also for listening to my class presentations, choir recital practices, and whatever else I needed help with when I was in school. Even though you weren't always able to help me with what I learned in school and didn't always understand English, I still appreciate how you did your best to help me through everything.

I'd like to also thank my friends, as always. Whether you're in Asia, Europe, Australia, or elsewhere in North America, I am so grateful for all of you. Thank you for being there for however long we were and/or are friends. Just like Mindy is lucky to have a friend like Sally, I am so fortunate to have friends like you.

To all the teachers, booksellers, parents, and librarians who encourage kids to read every day: thank you. I am the writer I am today because of the teachers, booksellers, librarians, et cetera, I met while growing up, so I know you're having an equally big impact on these children's lives. And to the parents who do their best for their children like my parents did for me: you're all rock stars. You inspire me daily with what you do, especially in the bumpy and uncertain year we've had.

Finally, I would like to thank everyone who is involved in the process of making the Mindy Kim books into a reality. Never in my wildest dreams could I have imagined having a children's book series of my own, and yet here we are now, releasing a fourth book of this series. What a wild and exciting journey it's been! Thank you for helping make my childhood dream into a reality. Fourth-grader Lyla would be so happy to know that dreams come true after all.

About the Author

Lyla Lee is the author of the Mindy Kim series as well as the YA novel *I'll Be the One*. Although she was born in a small town in South Korea, she's since then lived in various parts of the United States, including California, Florida, and Texas. Inspired by her English teacher, she started writing her own stories in fourth grade and finished her first novel at the age of fourteen. After working various jobs in Hollywood and studying psychology and cinematic arts at the University of Southern California, she now lives in Dallas, Texas. When she is not writing, she is teaching kids, petting cute dogs, and searching for the perfect bowl of shaved ice. You can visit her online at lylaleebooks.com.

Looking for another great book?
Find it
IN THE MIDDLE.

Fun, fantastic books for kids
in the in-be**TWEEN** age.

IntheMiddleBooks.com

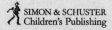 SIMON & SCHUSTER
Children's Publishing   /SimonKids   @SimonKids

Praise for
*Mindy Kim and the
Yummy Seaweed Business*

★ "A lovingly authentic debut
that shines."

—*Kirkus Reviews*, starred review

♥ Mindy Kim and the
Birthday Puppy ♥

**Don't miss more fun adventures
with Mindy Kim!**

*BOOK 1:
Mindy Kim and the Yummy Seaweed Business*

*BOOK 2:
Mindy Kim and the Lunar New Year Parade*

*BOOK 3:
Mindy Kim and the Birthday Puppy*

Coming soon:

*BOOK 4:
Mindy Kim, Class President*

Mindy Kim

and the
Birthday Puppy

BOOK

By Lyla Lee
Illustrated by Dung Ho

ALADDIN
New York London Toronto Sydney New Delhi

If you purchased this book without a cover, you should be aware that this book is stolen property. It was reported as "unsold and destroyed" to the publisher, and neither the author nor the publisher has received any payment for this "stripped book."

This book is a work of fiction. Any references to historical events, real people, or real places are used fictitiously. Other names, characters, places, and events are products of the author's imagination, and any resemblance to actual events or places or persons, living or dead, is entirely coincidental.

🕊 ALADDIN
An imprint of Simon & Schuster Children's Publishing Division
1230 Avenue of the Americas, New York, New York 10020
First Aladdin paperback edition May 2020
Text copyright © 2020 by Lyla Lee
Illustrations copyright © 2020 by Dung Ho
Also available in an Aladdin hardcover edition.
All rights reserved, including the right of reproduction in whole or in part in any form.
ALADDIN and related logo are registered trademarks of Simon & Schuster, Inc.
For information about special discounts for bulk purchases, please contact Simon & Schuster Special Sales at 1-866-506-1949 or business@simonandschuster.com.
The Simon & Schuster Speakers Bureau can bring authors to your live event. For more information or to book an event contact the Simon & Schuster Speakers Bureau at 1-866-248-3049 or visit our website at www.simonspeakers.com.
Designed by Laura Lyn DiSiena
The illustrations for this book were rendered digitally.
The text of this book was set in Haboro.
Manufactured in the United States of America 0420 OFF
10 9 8 7 6 5 4 3 2 1
Library of Congress Control Number 2020932432
ISBN 978-1-5344-4014-2 (hc)
ISBN 978-1-5344-4013-5 (pbk)
ISBN 978-1-5344-4015-9 (eBook)

For Lulu the Goldendoodle
and all the other dogs in my life.
You're the best!

♥ Mindy Kim and the
Birthday Puppy ♥

Chapter 1

My name is Mindy Kim. I am eight years old.

That's right—not seven, not seven and a half, but EIGHT.

Today is my birthday!

"Yay!" I jumped out of my bed with Mr. Toe Beans, my corgi stuffed doll.

The sun was shining bright outside, and even from inside my room, I could tell it was a beautiful day! And the best part? It was a Friday, and I was going to have a party after school with all my friends. I was so excited!

"Happy birthday, Mindy!" my dad said as he

opened my bedroom door. "How does it feel to be eight?"

I quickly hid Mr. Toe Beans behind my back before Dad could see. I was eight now! I didn't want Dad to think I still slept with a stuffed animal. Big kids didn't sleep with dolls, and the bigger of a kid I seemed, the more likely it was that Dad would buy me a puppy. Dad had said he'd get me a puppy for my birthday. And today was finally the day!

"Good! I feel so big now!"

Dad put a hand to his chin, like he was thinking really hard as he looked at me. "Hmm, you do seem a bit taller than you did yesterday."

"Really?" I bit my lip with excitement.

Dad laughed. "I'm just messing with you. But don't worry, sweetie. You're definitely still growing! Come down and eat some seaweed soup! Let's call your grandparents!"

Every birthday, I eat seaweed soup for breakfast. It's a Korean tradition! And then we call my grandparents in Korea so they can wish me happy birthday before they go to sleep. Korea time is thirteen hours ahead of Florida, so it was already nine p.m. there.

Mom used to always make seaweed soup for me, but since she wasn't here this year, Dad made it. It wasn't as good as Mom's, but I didn't tell him that. I didn't want to hurt his feelings.

Dad brought his laptop to the dining room table as I ate. Grandma and Grandpa were already on the screen, their smiles wide and eyes shining. They looked so happy to see me! And I was happy to see them, too.

"Saeng-il chook-ha-hae, Min-jung-ah!" said Grandpa, wishing me happy birthday in Korean. He used my Korean name, like everyone else did back in Korea.

"Gomap seum-nida!" I said thanks, bowing with respect.

My grandparents asked me a lot of questions about how I was doing and what I was going to do today. They always ask me lots of stuff when we talk, because we only call each other on special days. I don't know how to call my grandparents in

Korea by myself, and Dad is usually too busy to do it for me on regular days.

When we were done catching up, Dad put away his laptop and joined me at the table with his bowl of seaweed soup. I was done eating by then, but I remained sitting to keep Dad company.

"Dad," I asked, "why do we eat seaweed soup on our birthdays?"

"It's because a lot of mothers in Korea eat seaweed soup after they have their babies. Seaweed is full of nutrients that are really good for the moms."

Dad mentioning mothers reminded me of Mom and how she wasn't here to celebrate my birthday. And then I realized that she wasn't going to be here for any of my other birthdays, either. That made me really sad, all of a sudden.

"Are you excited for your party later today, Mindy?" Dad asked with a smile.

"Yes!" I said, trying to smile back.

Dad frowned, as if he knew what I was thinking. I'm a really bad liar.

"Your mom would be so proud of you, Mindy,"

he said. "It was hard, but you adjusted so well to living here. And you have so many friends now!"

"Thanks, Appa," I replied, feeling kind of grown-up.

I was looking forward to my party today, but I was also looking forward to getting a puppy for my birthday, just like my dad had said. But I didn't mention that part. I didn't want to ruin the surprise.

Chapter 2

At school, Mrs. Potts gave me a cute balloon that said IT'S MY BIRTHDAY TODAY! I also got to wear a gold paper crown on my head. I felt so special!

The class sang me "Happy Birthday," like we do for everyone's birthdays. I had a big smile the entire time they were singing. I felt so lucky and grateful!

"So, Mindy," Mrs. Potts said after they were done. "Before we get started with our class today, why don't you tell everyone what you plan on doing for your birthday?"

"I'm having a party!" I said. "And everyone in the class is invited!"

Several kids said "Yay!" and clapped with

7

excitement. Dad had already e-mailed the other parents about the party, so I knew not everyone could come, but I still wanted to say everyone was invited all the same.

"And," I added, "I think my dad is getting me a . . . puppy!"

The class gasped. Some kids even squealed!

"You *think*?" Mrs. Potts asked, looking confused.

"It's supposed to be a surprise, but I saw my dad looking at shelter websites on his tablet. And he said he would get me a puppy if I was grown-up and responsible enough!"

"Well, I'm wishing you the best today, Mindy," said Mrs. Potts. "I hope you have a wonderful day!"

Besides that morning, though, it was a pretty normal day of school. The only other thing that was different was that people who saw my golden crown in the hallway or in the cafeteria wished me happy birthday. When I first came to this school, I didn't think anyone would be nice to me, but now everyone was really friendly.

At recess, Sally let me have *two* turns on the swings. It made me so happy!

After I was done, I gave her a hug. "I'm so grateful you're my friend!"

Sally smiled. "I'm grateful you're my friend too!"

When school finally ended, I gathered up all my friends who were coming to my birthday party.

"I'll see everyone there! Be sure to come. We're going to have pizza, cake, and lots of fun games!"

I made sure everyone had the address to the park. Only Sally was coming in Dad's car with me, while the rest of my classmates had to find the way to the park themselves.

Dad came to pick me up. Eunice was riding in the shotgun seat. Eunice is my babysitter, and she's the one who usually picks me up from school. But not today. Dad had said he'd leave work early so he could set up for the party.

"Are you ready for the party, Mindy?" Dad asked with a big smile on his face.

"More than ready!"

Sally and I got into the back seat. I couldn't keep

still for the entire car ride. I was too excited for the party and the possibility of getting the puppy!

"I hope you like the decorations, Mindy," Dad said. "Julie and I have been hard at work since noon."

"Wow, Julie left work early to help out too?"

"Yup," Dad said. "She said she wanted to be there for your special day!"

Julie was my dad's new girlfriend. They'd just started officially dating a few weeks ago, but she was really nice and made Dad happy, so I liked her already!

On our way to the park, Sally whispered in my ear, "Hey, so do you really think you're getting a puppy today?"

"I hope so!" I whispered back. "It's all I want this year."

"I hope you get one too!" Sally replied. "What kind of dog do you want?"

I shrugged. I had favorite dog breeds, but when it came to actually getting a dog, I only cared about one thing.

"Whatever dog needs a good home!" I replied. "I've been looking at the dogs in the shelter for several months now, and every dog looks so cute but also really sad."

"Aw, yeah, shelter dogs always look so sad."

Just then I looked up, in time to see Dad glancing up at me in the rearview mirror! When our eyes met, though, he quickly glanced back to the road.

Could he hear Sally and me? Did this mean that he'd gotten me a puppy?

I had so many questions, and even though my heart was beating really fast, I didn't say anything. Hopefully, this would all be worth it in the end!

Chapter 3

When we got to the park, my jaw dropped open when I saw the picnic area. The trees around the picnic tables were decorated with pink and white balloons, while the tables themselves were covered with sky-blue tablecloths. Plates of yummy Korean food, pizza, and board games that everyone could play filled the tables. And that wasn't all! On one of the tables there was a huge mint chocolate chip ice cream cake with the words HAPPY BIRTHDAY, MINDY! written in pink frosting.

Julie and Mrs. Park, Eunice's mom, were finishing setting up. They gave us a wave when they saw Dad's car pull up to the parking space.

"Appa! Everything is so perfect!"

I gave Dad a big hug after we got out of the car. "Thank you so much!"

"You're welcome, Mindy," Dad said. "But I couldn't have done it alone, so be sure to thank Julie and Mrs. Park."

"Thank you so much!" I yelled with my hands cupped together.

Everyone laughed.

"I meant you should thank them when we're closer, but that works too," Dad said with a smile.

Sally and I jumped in to help prepare for the party before the guests arrived. We only had thirty minutes until people were supposed to start showing up! That seemed like a lot of time, but it wasn't when I thought about how much work we had to do.

As I was helping, I sneakily looked around for anything that could be a puppy. But the only presents on the table were much too small to be a puppy, unless Dad had gotten me a teacup Chihuahua.

I tried really hard not to be sad. Maybe I was wrong about a puppy after all.

Soon, though, the guests arrived, and I forgot about the puppy. We played lots of fun games, both Korean and American. We also played a big game of hide-and-seek in the playground and in the park! It was so fun!

When my party was almost over, Dad gathered everyone at the table with the cake.

"All right, everyone," he said. "It's time for cake and presents."

Everyone sang "Happy Birthday" to me, like they did in class. Only this time, some people got really into it. Dad sang into a spoon like he was singing karaoke! He was pretty off-key and made the people next to him wince, but it made me laugh. Dad was so funny.

Soon it was time for me to blow the candles out. It was official. I was really eight!

After that, I opened my presents. Everyone knew I liked dogs, so I got lots of new stuffed dogs and dog T-shirts. People also knew that I loved food, so they got me gift cards that I could spend on yummy things!

Although I was happy with my presents, with every box I opened, the more sure I became that I wasn't going to get a dog today. I was disappointed, but it was okay. Today was a perfect birthday, even without a puppy!

That's when I realized that Dad was nowhere to be found. I got really excited, and my hands started shaking so much that Sally had to help me open the next present. Could this mean what I thought it did?

Just then, Sally pointed and said, "Mindy, look over there!"

Everyone looked up and cheered.

Dad was coming our way with a really cute puppy. I wasn't sure what breed it was, but it didn't matter. To me, it was perfect. It had a big sky-blue bow on the back of its collar.

"Appa!" I squealed. "Is that *my* puppy?"

At the sound of my voice, the dog perked its ears and started running. I scooped it up and gave it a big hug, and it licked my face. I was so happy that I was crying.

People went "aww" as I gave Dad a big hug with the puppy smooshed in between us.

"Mindy, I know you've been wanting a dog for the longest time, and it is a lot of responsibility. But I think you're now ready."

"Don't worry, Dad," I said. "I promise to take good care of it and train it really well!"

"Plus, you can always ask me for help!" Eunice chimed in.

"And me!" Sally said. "You know we have two dogs at home."

"Thank you so much!" I replied to everyone.

I was so happy. This really was the perfect birthday!

Chapter 4

After everyone left and we finished cleaning up at the park, Dad and I went back home with my new four-legged friend. I checked to see if it was a boy or a girl. It was a boy puppy!

The shelter that Dad had adopted him from had given us a crate, and he was now in the crate to keep him safe during the drive. I held the crate tightly so it wouldn't slide around much. It could have just been my imagination, but he kind of looked grateful.

"Do you know what you're going to name him?" Dad asked.

I looked into the crate, where the puppy was

staring back at me with large, round eyes. He was trembling a little, like he was scared, but he still had a cute smile on his bushy face.

"Theodore!" I loudly declared. "Theodore the Mutt."

Dad laughed. "That's a peculiar name for a dog, Mindy."

I shrugged. "He just looks like a Theodore." It was because his bushy face kind of reminded of Teddy Roosevelt's mustache. We'd just learned about Theodore Roosevelt in class this week!

I didn't tell Dad, though. He'd probably think it was weird.

I was really excited to let Theodore out when we got home. He looked so lonely and sad in his crate!

"Are we close to home yet?" I asked Dad.

"We're five minutes away, Mindy," he replied. "Almost there."

"Okay."

I stuck my fingers into the crate so Theodore

would know I was right next to him. He licked my fingers! His tongue felt soft and wet. It tickled!

I giggled. "You're so sweet!"

Dad looked at me through the rearview mirror and smiled. "I'm so glad you two are getting along already!"

At home, Dad set Theodore's crate down on the floor and opened the door.

Theodore immediately dashed out of the crate, barking loudly as his paws clattered all over the floor.

"Whoa!" Dad exclaimed.

"Here, Theodore!" I said. "Come here, buddy!"

But Theodore just kept running around and barking. He jumped on the couch and knocked over Dad's favorite cushions, then dashed up the stairs, only to run down them again.

"Jeez, I hope he calms down," Dad said. "Maybe we can distract him with some of the treats I bought from the pet store."

"That's a great idea, Dad!"

Dad went back out to the car to grab the bag of treats from his car. Alone in the house, I tried my best to get Theodore's attention.

"Theodore! Hey, buddy! Calm down!"

But it was no use. The dog just kept running. He got a hold of the blanket on the couch and started pulling on it.

I took the other end of the blanket and started pulling it, too. Theodore wagged his tail, like he thought it was a game.

"No!" I said. "Bad dog!"

I tried to wrestle the blanket away from him, but it was no use. And then the worst thing happened. The blanket tore!

At that moment, Dad came back with the bag of treats.

"Oh no!" He exclaimed. "That blanket was your mom's!"

He looked really sad, and I felt terrible. I was also really afraid, because this was Theodore's first day at home and he'd already caused trouble. The way Dad was looking at Theodore was not good. He looked kind of mad!

"Theodore, come here!" Dad said in a very firm voice. It was the voice he used when I was in big trouble.

Dad opened the bag of treats, and it was like magic. Theodore let go of the torn blanket right in front of Dad and stared up at him while panting with his tongue out.

I took a treat from the bag and waved it in front of Theodore.

"Sit!"

The puppy didn't do anything.

"Hmm," Dad said. "I guess he isn't trained yet. Are you up for training him, Mindy?"

He was still looking at the torn blanket, and I got really nervous. What if Theodore continued to be bad, and Dad returned him to the shelter?

I tightly squeezed my fists. I couldn't let that happen, no matter what.

"I sure am!" I said really loudly. I was determined to make Theodore the best behaved and best trained dog ever. That way, Dad wouldn't even *think* about returning poor Theodore to the shelter!

After trying to make him sit a few more times, I gave Theodore the treat anyway. At least he wasn't running around the house anymore!

By then it was bedtime, and since Theodore wasn't potty trained yet, Dad had to put him back inside his crate.

"I'll see you in the morning, Theodore," I whispered, putting my face up against the door of the crate. "Good night!"

As soon as Dad and I went up the stairs, Theodore started whimpering.

"We're just going to have to ignore him for now, Mindy," Dad said. "He can sleep with you on your bed after he's house-trained!"

After Dad had tucked me in and gone back downstairs, I tried to ignore Theodore's cries like Dad said I should. But his voice was really loud, and he sounded so sad!

I wanted to cry.

It's okay, Theodore! I thought. *Soon I'll teach*

you how to be a good dog so you can come sleep in my room!

Tomorrow was a Saturday, which meant I could spend a lot of time with Theodore. I was determined to make him the best-behaved dog ever!

Chapter 5

The next day, Eunice came over to help me potty train Theodore.

"Okay," she said. "So, the first thing you need to know about puppies is that they have very small bladders. That means they have to go potty all the time. Since you're at school and your dad has to go to work, you should probably put Theodore in the bathroom with puppy pads so he can go when no one's home. And you have to train him so he knows he should go on the pads. I'll show you how!"

Eunice and I went over to where Theodore already was, in the bathroom. We were keeping him in a pen in the bathroom for now, since it was too mean to have him locked up in the crate all day, and Dad said he didn't want him to roam around the house until he was trained. I think he was scared Theodore might make a mess like last night.

Theodore stood at the edge of the pen and stared at us with his large eyes as he wagged his tail.

We just stared back at him. When we didn't do anything for a while, he whined and whimpered.

"So, we just watch him until he goes?" I guessed. "And then give him a treat?"

"Well, just for the first time, yeah. You can go do something else for a few hours after that . . . probably two or three. Until he needs to go again. Then try to get him to go on the pads, and if he does, give him another treat!"

While we were waiting for Theodore to pee, Eunice and I watched a Korean drama on her phone. Korean dramas are Korean TV shows. My mom and I used to watch them together all the time, but I hadn't watched any since she died.

The one Eunice picked was about a girl who

falls in love with an alien. It was kind of weird, but it was funny, too!

Soon enough, Theodore had to pee, and he peed on one of the pads!

"Good boy!" I cheered, and gave him a treat. He looked so happy while he ate!

"And that's it!" Eunice said. "Keep doing this and he'll probably be house-trained within two weeks. Don't get mad at him if he doesn't pee on the pad, though. Because then he'll sneak around the house and keep having accidents."

"Okay!" I said. It seemed easy enough!

After Eunice left, Dad let me use his tablet so I could look up how to train Theodore to do other things. That seemed pretty straightforward too! All I had to do was give Theodore a treat whenever he did what I told him to do.

I was so excited! I was going to train Theodore to do all kinds of cool stuff, like dance and play dead! It was going to be easy-peasy.

After dinner, I went back into the bathroom to hang out with Theodore.

I held out a treat in front of me as I pointed at the floor.

"Theodore, sit!"

Theodore just stared back at me.

"Sit, boy! Sit, Theodore!"

I tried a couple more times, but it was no use. I thought long and hard about what to do. And then I got an idea.

I approached Theodore, and this time I slowly moved my hand above his head so he had to back away from me. "Theodore, sit!"

It worked! As he backed away, Theodore sat down to make space for me.

"Good boy!"

Like Eunice said I should do, I gave Theodore the treat. He happily munched on it before standing up again.

I tried making him sit again. This time, it only took two more tries before Theodore sat down.

"Good boy! You're so smart!"

That night, I said good-bye to Theodore before I went to bed again.

"You're doing so great, buddy!" I said. "Soon you'll be completely trained and an expert in dog manners. And then you can go wherever you want in the house."

Theodore whined and whimpered again throughout the night, and I hugged Mr. Shiba, my Shiba Inu stuffed doll, tight.

I couldn't wait for the day I could sleep in my bed with my real dog!

Chapter 6

After teaching Theodore some more training basics, Dad and I decided to take him to a dog park. He was starting to look lonely all by himself at home.

The dog park was in a fenced area with lots of trees. There were a ton of dogs already playing in the park, including a golden retriever, a corgi, a husky, and a Westie! All the big dogs were on one side of the park, while the small dogs were on the other. They were separated by a big fence.

"It's so the big dogs don't hurt the little dogs," Dad explained when I asked him about the fence.

All the dogs were so cute! I couldn't wait to say

hi to everyone! And I couldn't wait for Theodore to become friends with them.

"Look, Theodore!" I said. "So many friends!"

I glanced down at him, expecting him to be wagging his tail. Instead Theodore was hiding behind me with his tail tucked between his hind legs.

"Aw, what's wrong, buddy?"

I knelt down so I was face to face with Theodore. He was shaking. He looked really scared!

"Hey," I said softly, patting him on the head. "It's okay. I'm sure the dogs are really nice! You'll go on the side with the small dogs, so it'll be okay! Dad and I will keep you safe, I promise!"

But Theodore still looked scared. When I tried to lead him toward the dog park, he tugged the opposite way on his leash.

Suddenly I wasn't so sure if this was a good idea. Theodore's ears drooped a little, and the sad look in his eyes reminded me of how scared I was on the first day at my new school.

"Being the new kid is always hard, but you can

do it!" I said. "I believe in you! Let's go make new friends!"

I started running toward the park, and Theodore followed me.

"Wait, Mindy!" Dad said. "Slow down or you'll get the other dogs too riled up."

I looked up to see that Dad was right. The dogs that'd been playing near the gate stopped to stare at us. A few of the mean-looking ones started to bark!

More slowly this time, Dad and I led Theodore to the gate of the dog park. As soon as we went inside, the Westie came over, wagging its tail.

"Look, Theodore, a new friend! Be sure to play nice!"

But before Theodore could sniff the other dog, another dog–a Maltese–started yapping and snapping at him!

Theodore yelped and ran back to hide behind me.

I waved at the barking Maltese.

"Go away, you little pipsqueak! Leave Theodore alone!"

"Sorry!" said a fancy-looking lady as she came running over to us. "No, Priscilla!" she said to the Maltese. "Bad girl!"

She scooped the tiny dog into her arms and walked away from us.

The Westie came closer again, sniffing around Theodore. But this time Theodore shrank back and froze until the dog left.

Dad sighed. "Mindy, I don't think Theodore is ready to make friends yet. It doesn't seem like he's good with other dogs."

"He's just shy!" I said. "He only needs a bit of encouragement!"

It made me really sad that Theodore was having so much trouble making friends. If only he weren't so afraid of other dogs!

I gently reached behind me and gave Theodore a little shove. "Go play, boy!"

After a few more shoves, Theodore went off running and made a few laps of the park. The other dogs started chasing Theodore.

"That's it! Play!"

But then a shih tzu snapped at him, and Theodore yelped.

"Theodore, no!"

The other dogs ran away when I bolted toward them. "Leave him alone!"

When I scooped him into my arms, Theodore was shaking so much. I felt really bad for pushing him.

A very tall man came toward us.

"Hey, sorry, guys," he said. "But honestly, your dog doesn't look like he's having any fun. You should take him back home."

I expected Dad to tell the man he was being really rude. But instead Dad didn't say anything. He frowned as the man walked away and then said again, "I don't think he's ready, Mindy. We should leave before something bad happens."

The other dogs were watching Theodore now. Their owners looked really wary too. I was so sad. Why couldn't everyone be nicer to Theodore? He was the new kid!

I put the leash back on Theodore and led him out of the fenced area.

"It's okay, Theodore," I said. "We can try again another day."

Chapter 7

Back home, Dad and I decided Theodore needed a bath. It was going to be his first one! I did my research, and the Internet said we should fill the tub so it went halfway up Theodore's legs and make sure that Theodore didn't get water in his ears.

My bathtub was too small for the three of us, so Dad and I took Theodore to the master bathroom. Dad got in the bath first and made sure the water wasn't too hot for Theodore or me.

"Okay, I think it's ready!" he said after a few minutes.

I picked up Theodore and carefully got into the bath with him. Dad and I were both wearing shorts, so the water didn't make our clothes wet.

Gently, I lowered Theodore into the water. The moment he touched the water, his ears flattened against his head and he whimpered.

"I guess he doesn't like water," Dad said. "That's too bad. I heard some dogs like to swim."

The thought of Theodore swimming made me giggle. He was so small that it was hard to imagine him bravely moving in the water. Maybe he could when he was more grown-up!

Theodore was trembling from head to toe. He looked really scared.

"It's okay, buddy," I said. "It's just water!"

Gently, I scooped a handful of the lukewarm water and lightly splashed it on him. He sniffed my still-wet hand and licked it. It tickled!

Dad and I carefully splashed water on Theodore until his entire body was wet. Damp, Theodore looked really funny, and he was a lot skinnier, too! He looked more like a big mouse than a dog.

Dad put some oatmeal-scented dog shampoo onto his hands and scrubbed it into Theodore's fur.

Theodore stood still, and even closed his eyes a little bit.

I giggled. "He's liking your massage, Dad!"

Dad smiled. It was the first time I'd seen him smile because of Theodore!

I reached out and helped spread the shampoo all over Theodore. He was still shaking, but luckily, he was keeping still. He was being such a good boy!

"Good boy, Theodore!" I said. "I'll give you a brand-new bone after this. You totally deserve one!"

He wagged his tail, like he knew what I was saying. Dad and I grinned at each other.

Even though taking care of him was a lot of work, Theodore was so cute that it was all worth it. And I was really glad I had Dad by my side to help me!

Chapter 8

Monday I had to go back to school. Saying good-bye to Theodore was so hard! I gave him a big hug before Dad and I left the house.

"He'll be fine, Mindy. Don't worry," said Dad. "You'll be back home before you know it."

When I started closing the bathroom door, Theodore lay down on the floor and stared up at me with sad eyes.

"I'll be back soon, buddy," I said. "I promise!"

The school day seemed really long, a thousand billion times longer than usual. I kept staring at the clock on the classroom wall.

During lunch, everyone who was at my birthday party asked me about my puppy.

"What did you name him?" Dill wanted to know.

"Theodore!"

"Theodore?" Dill asked. "Why did you name him that?"

I shrugged. "He looked like a Theodore! Kind of like Teddy Roosevelt."

Everyone at my table giggled.

"Well, I think the name is perfect and cute," Sally said. I could always count on her to have my back! "How is potty training going?"

I told my friends all about my weekend with Theodore.

"You should give him peanut butter when he's a good boy!" said Dill. "Dogs love peanut butter!"

"But don't give him chocolate. It's poisonous."

"Get a bell chain and hang it on the doorknob so he can ring the bell whenever he needs to go potty outside!"

Everyone had such good tips! But then some

people had really silly suggestions like:

"Throw him in the water and it'll teach him how to swim!"

"Wear a mask and run around while chasing him!"

The boys who suggested this laughed and high-fived each other.

Sally rolled her eyes. "Ugh," she said. "Don't listen to them. They're just being silly."

My friends who couldn't make it to my party said they wanted to see what Theodore looked like. I promised I would bring pictures for our next "What's New with You?" show-and-tell!

After school, Eunice picked me up and drove me back to my house. I was bouncing up and down in my seat during the entire car ride.

Eunice laughed. "I was like that when we first got Oliver, too! The first day away is always hard."

Oliver the Maltese is Eunice's dog. He and I are buddies, even though he only pays attention to me when I have food.

When we arrived, Theodore was so glad to see me that he peed on the floor!

"Gross!" Eunice exclaimed. "It's okay. A lot of puppies do that. Hopefully, he'll grow out of it."

After we cleaned up the mess, we got Theodore's leash so we could take him out for a walk. Eunice told me to pack some treats before we left.

"What do we need those for?" I asked.

Eunice smiled. "You'll see."

Theodore wasn't good at walking with a leash yet. His little legs moved so fast that they became a blur. He tugged and tugged until he coughed because the collar was choking him.

"No, boy, slow down! You're choking yourself!" I said. "Slow down!"

"Here, let me," said Eunice. "The trick is to stop whenever he pulls and only keep going when he calms down. It takes a lot of patience, but he'll get it eventually!"

When Eunice started walking, Theodore wiggled and strained against his leash. Eunice stopped and stood still until he gave up. Only when he was completely still did she start walking again, all the while showing him the treat.

"Okay, now you try," Eunice said, handing me the leash.

"Okay!"

Like Eunice did, I started walking but stopped when he pulled again. It was a really slow process, but I was determined to train Theodore so he could walk with a leash!

We did one loop around the neighborhood park before heading back home.

As we walked, I told Eunice about Theodore's rough day at the dog park. When I was done telling her everything, she said, "I have an idea! How about we introduce him to Oliver? He's pretty nice to other dogs. I think it's because he's a bit older."

"That'd be so great!" I said.

Theodore had another chance to make a friend!

Chapter 9

The next day, after school, I scooped Theodore into my arms and got into Eunice's car. Theodore was scared of riding in the car, but I gave him a tight hug.

"It's okay, boy. Eunice doesn't live far from us, so it'll be a short ride!"

Theodore licked my face. He was so sweet!

Even before we entered Eunice's house, Oliver started barking. His little yips were so loud that we could hear them from outside.

Theodore started barking too. His voice was a little lower but more babyish.

"They're talking to each other already!" I said. I hoped this meant they would become friends really soon.

We walked up to Eunice's door. When she opened it, Oliver shot out of the house, raced around the yard, and then ran back toward us in a white blur!

Theodore yelped and jumped behind me.

"It's okay, Theodore! Oliver just wants to say hi!"

Oliver reached us, and soon he was chasing Theodore. The two dogs ran in circles around me. They were making me dizzy!

Eunice waited for the right moment and then quickly scooped Oliver into her arms.

"Gotcha!" she said.

The small dog squirmed around.

"Here," she said. "Maybe this will help."

She carried Oliver into the house, and Theodore and I followed after her. Once we were all inside, Eunice sat on the living room floor, still hugging Oliver close to her.

I gave Theodore a gentle shove.

"Okay," she said. "Now Theodore should be able to properly meet Oliver."

"Go say hi!"

Theodore sniffed my hands, then cautiously moved toward Oliver. Oliver stuck his head out in Theodore's direction and started barking again.

Theodore froze, and his tail went between his legs.

"It's okay, buddy!" I said. "Oliver is nice!"

I softly pushed Theodore again. He slowly approached Oliver again, sniffing the floor.

And then, finally, Oliver and Theodore were nose to nose!

I crossed my fingers and toes and held my breath as the two dogs sniffed each other. I really hoped they'd get along! Oliver squirmed around in Eunice's grip, but she held tight.

Theodore started wagging his tail, and so did Oliver. So far, so good.

And then Eunice slowly let go of Oliver. This time Oliver didn't run. And neither did Theodore. The two dogs continued sniffing each other, looking really excited. They even sniffed each other's butts!

Eunice and I laughed.

"It's so funny when dogs do that," Eunice said. "It's the dog way of saying hi. Let's find a ball so they can play with each other!"

Eunice picked up a tennis ball that was in the corner of the room. She handed it to me.

"Try throwing it!"

"Okay!" I turned to the dogs. "Theodore! Oliver!"

I waved the ball in front of me. Both dogs turned to look at me, their eyes wide with attention.

I giggled. They were both so cute!

"Wait!" Eunice took out her phone and snapped a picture of the dogs.

"Good thinking!" I said. I couldn't wait to show the picture to Dad!

I circled my arm around and around, like I'd seen baseball pitchers do on TV.

"Ready . . . set . . . go!"

I threw the ball. The two dogs burst into action, their paws skittering across the wooden floor as they ran after it. Theodore and Oliver were about the same size, but Theodore was much faster. He caught the ball! I was so proud.

Oliver ran after Theodore and chased him across the house. Only this time Theodore didn't look afraid. He was having fun!

"It looks like they're getting along!" Eunice said. "That's a relief."

"Yay!"

Eunice got out one of Oliver's tug-of-war toys. "Let's see if they'll play with this!"

She held the toy in front of Oliver, who immediately grabbed the other end. She then gave her end to Theodore. The two dogs growled and played with each other. It was so cute!

We watched the dogs play together for a little while longer, until we got kind of hungry.

"Hey, want some snacks?" Eunice asked. "My mom bought some shrimp crackers from the Korean market. We can snack on them while we continue watching the Korean drama we watched this weekend!"

"Okay! Sounds fun!"

While the dogs kept playing, Eunice and I curled up on her living room couch with the shrimp crackers and watched the Korean drama. While we were laughing at the show together, I thought about how—even though she's my babysitter—Eunice was the first friend I made here in Florida. And until now, Theodore had had no friends, but now he was friends with Oliver!

I was so grateful that Theodore and I had friends like Oliver and Eunice!

Chapter 10

The next day at school, we had to draw our family portrait during art class. At first I was nervous, because everyone at my table was drawing their mom and their dad. I was afraid Dad and I would look lonely.

"What's wrong, Mindy?" asked Sally when she saw that I wasn't drawing anything.

I looked over at her paper. She'd drawn her big, happy family, with her two older sisters, her mom, and her dad. My family would look so small compared to hers!

I was a little sad. But then I got an idea.

I raised my hand.

"Yes, Mindy?" said Mr. Stephenson, the art teacher.

"Can I include my dog in my family portrait? His name is Theodore, and he's an important part of my family!"

A few people in the class giggled. Mr. Stephenson smiled.

"Well, of course, Mindy! Dogs and other pets are definitely important parts of our families. I encourage everyone to include their pets in their drawings!"

The class cheered. Everyone around me started to add their pets into their drawings. There were lots of cute dogs, but also a bunch of other animals too, like cats, hamsters, bunnies, and turtles. Some people even drew their fish!

I drew Theodore first, and then Dad and me. I decided to draw a picture of us in the bathtub, giving Theodore a bath! Getting all three of us in the bathtub was hard, but I made it work.

For Dad and me, I drew smiley faces. I wasn't sure if a smiley face would look good on a dog, so I made Theodore's tongue stick out.

Mr. Stephenson came over to look at my work.

"A family portrait in the bathtub! How creative!" He laughed. "Everyone is so happy!"

I looked down at my drawing and smiled. We *did* look happy! And we were.

Dad, Theodore, and I were our own happy family!

Chapter 11

When Eunice and I got home from school, Theodore greeted us at the door. He jumped and barked. He was so happy to see me! He jumped so much that he knocked me over to the floor.

"Hmm," said Eunice. "It's nice that he's so friendly, but we really need to teach him to not jump on people like that. How about we teach him a few more tricks after we finish our homework?"

"Sure!"

I finished my homework as fast as I could. We were doing fractions and decimals. I liked fractions and decimals! They were much better compared to my greatest enemy: long division.

After I was done, Eunice checked my answers for any silly mistakes.

"Looks good!" she said. "I'm all set with my homework too. I'll help you teach Theodore a few tricks before I go!"

The first trick we wanted to teach Theodore was "down." Eunice told me to give Theodore a little piece of a treat whenever he went down on all fours instead of jumping on me.

I held a treat out so Theodore could see it. He got really excited and started jumping up and down, trying to get the treat.

"No," I said. "Down. Down!"

"You have to say it more firmly," Eunice said. "Say it like a scary teacher!"

I tried my best to sound like Dr. Mortimer, our scary principal. "Down!"

I softly brushed Theodore off my legs so he was sitting down on the floor.

"Quick!" said Eunice. "Give him a treat now!"

I gave Theodore the treat. But when I got out a new treat, he jumped again.

"It'll probably take a couple more tries," Eunice said. "It's okay, though. He'll get it eventually!"

Dad came home, and Eunice left. At the dinner table, I was so antsy. I wanted to go back to training Theodore so that Dad could see he was a good dog!

"Hey, Mindy. Julie is going to come over for dinner on Friday. Would that be okay with you?"

"Sure!"

Now that Julie was coming over, I *really* wanted to teach Theodore to do a bunch of tricks. Then we could impress Dad *and* Julie at the same time! It was going to be tough, but I had faith in Theodore and me.

"Dad, can I use your tablet?" I said. "I want to look up the best ways to train Theodore!"

"Sure, but be careful not to feed him too many treats, Mindy," said Dad. "We don't want him to be overfed and get a stomachache."

"I won't. I promise!"

There were lots of videos on YouTube on how to train a dog. It was pretty confusing, but I decided to give it a shot!

At first Theodore was really confused too. When I held a treat above him, he jumped and bit my hand!

"Ow!" I said. "No! Bad dog."

Theodore flattened his ears and looked really sorry.

I petted him. "It's okay. I know you didn't mean to hurt me."

Theodore and I went over "down" a few more times. It took him fifteen tries, but at the end he went down when I told him to!

"Good boy!" I said. I was so proud of him! It took him a while, but he got it in the end.

I wanted to teach Theodore a few more tricks, but I was tired. I'd had enough of dog training for today.

At that moment, Dad popped his head into the living room.

"It's time for bed, Mindy," he said.

"Okay," I said.

I looked down at Theodore, who was looking at me with expectant eyes.

"We'll just have to try again tomorrow, Theodore," I said. "I'll teach you how to shake hands and all sorts of other cool stuff by Friday!"

Theodore wagged his tail.

The truth was, after today, I wasn't sure Theodore could learn all those things in time. But as Dad liked to say, "Hope for the best and it'll all work out."

I told Theodore this, and he wagged his tail again.

Chapter 12

The next day, I finished my homework fast so I could have lots of time to train Theodore.

Training Theodore was harder than I thought it would be, but it was still worth it. He tried so hard, and even though it sometimes took him a lot of times to get something right, I loved him so much for trying his best.

On Friday, Dad came home early to prepare dinner. We were making bulgogi and bibimbap! Bulgogi is a yummy Korean barbecue beef dish, while bibimbap is rice mixed with egg, vegetables, and gochujang, a spicy pepper paste.

The bibimbap was easy because all Dad had to

do was mix in the sliced vegetables from the Korean market with the spicy pepper paste, eggs, and rice. And Dad had already marinated the meat for the bulgogi, so he just had to cook it.

While Dad heated up the meat on the stove, I helped by putting all the ingredients of the bibim-bap into three separate bowls. And Theodore? Well, Theodore couldn't really help, but he walked around following everybody!

He sniffed the air and looked really happy.

"Can we give Theodore some of the meat?" I asked Dad.

"I don't think we should," he replied. "Marinated meat is really bad for dogs."

I couldn't meet Theodore's eyes after that. I felt so bad that he couldn't have any of the meat!

After the meat was done cooking, Dad fried the eggs on the stove and placed them on the bibim-bap with some sesame seeds and sesame oil as a finishing touch.

Then we put the bowls of bibimbap and the plate of bulgogi on the dining room table and gave each other a high five. Dad and I were master chefs!

When Julie came, she sniffed the air appreciatively.

"Wow! The food smells so good!" she exclaimed. "I didn't know you were such a good cook, Brian!"

Dad blushed. "I couldn't have done it without Mindy. She helped a lot."

"I sure did!" I said. "But Dad is getting better every day. When we first moved here, he couldn't even reheat dumplings without hurting himself!"

Julie laughed.

Dad looked embarrassed, but he still said, "Aw, thank you, Mindy."

Dinner was so tasty that everyone was in a good mood. Theodore rested his head on my knees while I ate. I wanted to sneak him some food so bad! But I didn't want to hurt him, so I didn't. I hoped he wouldn't hate me for it.

When we were done eating, Dad said, "Mindy and Theodore have something to show us. Right, Mindy?"

I nodded as I got out of my seat and tried not to

look nervous. "Yup! Come here, Theodore!"

Theodore got up, his ears perked and head cocked to the side with attention.

I got some dog treats and went to the living room with Theodore. Dad and Julie sat on the couch to give us their undivided attention.

"First," I said, "the easy-peasy part."

I held a treat in front of me and touched my shoulder with the other hand. "Theodore, sit!"

Theodore blinked up at me, wagging his tail slightly. He sat down.

Dad and Julie clapped.

"Woo-hoo! Go, Theodore!" I cheered.

Theodore's tail went faster, like he knew they were cheering for him. I gave him a treat.

"Okay. Next: Theodore, down."

I pointed at the floor.

Theodore got down flat against the floor.

"Good boy!" I gave him another treat.

"Wow, what a smart dog!" Julie said.

I grinned. "We're only halfway there!"

I turned back to Theodore, who'd gotten back up on his feet. "Okay, Theodore."

I rested a hand in front of him. "Paw!"

Theodore stared at my hand and then at the treat. I held my breath.

Come on boy, I thought. *You can do it!*

He put his paw on my hand.

"Outstanding!" hooted Dad.

"Last but not least . . ." After Theodore had gotten back up on his feet, I bounced the treat up and down above his head. "Dance!"

But instead of dancing, Theodore jumped up.

"No, boy," I said. "Not jump. Dance!"

I tried again.

This time Theodore stared up at my hand. He looked really confused.

"It's okay, Mindy," Dad said. "Maybe that trick is too hard for Theodore."

I shook my head. "No, he can do it. Watch!"

I tried for a third time.

Theodore got up on his hind legs and bounced

up and down like he was supposed to!

Dad and Julie got to their feet and clapped while they cheered. It was a standing ovation!

"Amazing!" said Dad.

"What a good boy!" said Julie.

I gave Theodore a treat and then hugged him. I was so proud of him! It wasn't easy, but we did it!

Chapter 13

That night, Dad tucked Theodore and me into bed. Theodore was pretty good with potty training now, so Dad said he could finally sleep with me in my room!

"You did such a wonderful job training Theodore, Mindy," said Dad. "You've just turned eight, but you're so much more responsible already!"

"I wanted to prove to you that Theodore was a good dog!" I said. "The Internet says that all dogs can be trained, even rescues! People just don't give them a chance."

Dad nodded. "You are so right, Mindy. I see that now. I'm sorry I doubted you and Theodore."

He reached over to give Theodore a pat on the head.

Just then, I remembered my drawing. Mr. Stephenson had given me a gold star for it, but I'd forgotten to take it out of my backpack until now.

"Appa, I want to show you something."

"Oh? What is it, Mindy?"

I got up from my bed and gently pulled my drawing from my backpack. It was a little wrinkly, but that was okay.

"We had to draw a family portrait for art class," I said. "And this is what I drew!"

Dad's eyes went wide as he looked at his portrait. "We look so happy!"

"That's what Mr. Stephenson said too! And I agree."

Dad carefully took the drawing from me like it was the most expensive drawing in the entire world. He held it in front of his face and stared even more closely at it. "I'm going to frame this and hang it up. This is a really nice drawing, Mindy. Thank you for sharing it with me."

I beamed with pride. "You're welcome!"

"The three of us really are a happy family, aren't we?" Dad said, sounding thoughtful. His eyes looked a little shiny as he smiled.

"Yup!"

"I'm so grateful for you, Mindy," Dad said. "And you too, Theodore."

He gave Theodore another pat on the head. Theodore wagged his tail.

"I love you, Dad," I said.

"I love you too, Mindy. And . . . yes, you too, Theodore. Now good night, you two."

Dad turned off the lights and left my room, still carefully holding the drawing.

I petted Theodore.

"You hear that, Theodore? Dad said he loves you. And *I* love you even more! You are so loved!"

Theodore licked my hand, and I giggled.

This was the beginning of a beautiful friendship.

Acknowledgments

First and foremost, I'd like to thank my parents, who got me a puppy for my tenth birthday and made my childhood dream come true. This book is largely based on that experience, even though Mindy is only eight when she gets her dog. (Lucky duck!)

I would next like to thank all the teachers, librarians, booksellers, and students I met while I was on tour over the past year. Thank you so much for loving Mindy and for accepting her into your hearts. Mindy is really lucky to have friends like you!

Thank you also to all the parents who bought the Mindy Kim books and/or reached out to me over social media to tell me how much their kids are loving Mindy. Your messages always brighten my world, even on my worst days. Thank you for sharing the Mindy Kim series and other books with your kids to foster their love of reading. You're all rock stars.

Like any book I write, this book wouldn't have been possible without the support of my friends, who remind me to take care of myself and have fun whenever life gets stressful. Thank you for hanging out with me and for making my last couple of months a little bit brighter. I already mentioned most of them in my previous books, but here's a special shout-out to Chelsea Chang, Shiyun Sun, Luke Chou, Bernice Yau, Alice Zhu, Steven Bell, Sherry Yang, Kelly Huang, Kaiti Liu, and Stephanie Liu. A whole other separate mention goes to Aneeqah Naeem, who's once again sitting across the table from me as I write this. I consider myself really fortunate to have friends like you.

Lastly, thank you always to Alyson Heller, Penny Moore, Cassie Malmo, and Jenny Lu. Thank you for all that you do to support Mindy and me. We're so lucky to have a team like you! And of course, thank you to Dung Ho for her always spot-on illustrations that bring Mindy and her adventures to life.

**Don't miss Mindy's
next adventure!**

About the Author

Lyla Lee is the author of the Mindy Kim series as well as the upcoming YA novel *I'll Be the One*. Although she was born in a small town in South Korea, she's since then lived in various parts of the United States, including California, Florida, and Texas. Inspired by her English teacher, she started writing her own stories in fourth grade and finished her first novel at the age of fourteen. After working various jobs in Hollywood and studying psychology and cinematic arts at the University of Southern California, she now lives in Dallas, Texas. When she is not writing, she is teaching kids, petting cute dogs, and searching for the perfect bowl of shaved ice. You can visit her online at lylaleebooks.com.

♥ **Mindy Kim and the
Lunar New Year Parade** ♥

**Don't miss more fun adventures
with Mindy Kim!**

BOOK 1:
Mindy Kim and the Yummy Seaweed Business

BOOK 2:
Mindy Kim and the Lunar New Year Parade

Coming soon:

BOOK 3:
Mindy Kim and the Birthday Puppy

Mindy Kim

and the
Lunar New Year
Parade

BOOK
2

By Lyla Lee

Illustrated by Dung Ho

ALADDIN

New York London Toronto Sydney New Delhi

If you purchased this book without a cover, you should be aware that this book is stolen property. It was reported as "unsold and destroyed" to the publisher, and neither the author nor the publisher has received any payment for this "stripped book."

This book is a work of fiction. Any references to historical events, real people, or real places are used fictitiously. Other names, characters, places, and events are products of the author's imagination, and any resemblance to actual events or places or persons, living or dead, is entirely coincidental.

ALADDIN
An imprint of Simon & Schuster Children's Publishing Division
1230 Avenue of the Americas, New York, New York 10020
First Aladdin paperback edition January 2020
Text copyright © 2020 by Lyla Lee
Illustrations copyright © 2020 by Dung Ho
Also available in an Aladdin hardcover edition.
All rights reserved, including the right of reproduction in whole or in part in any form.
ALADDIN and related logo are registered trademarks of Simon & Schuster, Inc.
For information about special discounts for bulk purchases, please contact Simon & Schuster Special Sales at 1-866-506-1949 or business@simonandschuster.com.
The Simon & Schuster Speakers Bureau can bring authors to your live event. For more information or to book an event contact the Simon & Schuster Speakers Bureau at 1-866-248-3049 or visit our website at www.simonspeakers.com.
Book designed by Laura Lyn DiSiena
The illustrations for this book were rendered digitally.
The text of this book was set in Haboro.
Manufactured in the United States of America 1219 OFF
10 9 8 7 6 5 4 3 2 1
Library of Congress Control Number 2019948664
ISBN 978-1-5344-4011-1 (hc)
ISBN 978-1-5344-4010-4 (pbk)
ISBN 978-1-5344-4012-8 (eBook)

To my parents, who always kept me connected
to my Korean culture

Mindy Kim and the
Lunar New Year Parade

Chapter 1

My name is Mindy Kim.

I'm almost eight years old, or at least, that's how old I am in the United States. In Korea, though, I'm nine! That's what Dad told me as he drove me to school.

"Korean people calculate age differently," he said. "You're already one year old when you're born, and then you get one year older on New Year's Day, instead of getting older on your birthday."

I got really excited, since it's been eight years since I was born. One plus eight is nine, and nine years old was *definitely* old enough to get a puppy.

And even better yet, Lunar New Year was this Saturday!

"Does this mean that I'll turn ten this weekend?" I asked, throwing my backpack in the back seat.

Dad laughed. "No, silly. People only age up on the first of January *or* on Lunar New Year, not both."

I sat back into my seat with a big huff. "What's

the point of two New Years if you can only age up on one?"

Dad shook his head as he pulled into the school's parking lot. "It's an important part of our culture, Mindy. It goes way back to the times when our ancestors in Korea used the lunar calendar to tell time. Tell you what, why don't we go to the Lunar New Year parade in Orlando this weekend? I saw an ad for it the other day. It looks like it'll be fun!"

Dad smiled at me, but I was unconvinced. The last time Dad said something would be "fun," I ended up watching a boring show about really slow slugs all by myself because he fell asleep in five minutes.

Plus, so much has changed since the last time we celebrated Lunar New Year. Last year, Dad, Mom, and I celebrated with the other Korean people in our neighborhood. We played really fun games like yutnori and jegichagi, ate so many yummy rice cakes, and even sang karaoke! There was no way that we could have as much fun this year as we did then.

Not without Mom.

Now the only other Korean family in our neighborhood is Eunice's, and they were going to Seattle to visit their relatives for the holiday. It was just going to be me and Dad.

"The parade will be fun," Dad said again. "It'll be good for us to leave the house."

I sighed. Dad really wanted to go to the parade! And I didn't want to make him sad by saying I didn't want to go.

"Okay," I said. "I'll go to the parade."

Dad beamed. "Great! See you after school, honey."

"Bye, Appa," I said, using the Korean word for "Daddy."

I headed toward the school, my shoulders slumped. I was not looking forward to Lunar New Year. Not anymore.

Chapter 2

After school was over, Eunice picked me up like usual. But since Dad was working super late today, she took us to her house instead of going to mine.

"So, Mindy, are you excited for Lunar New Year?" Eunice asked while we were doing homework in her room.

"Not really," I said. "We're not really doing anything. Just going to a parade in Orlando."

"Ooh, parades are fun, though! I heard the Orlando one is really good. It got so popular that they had to move it to a larger location to fit all the people!"

"I wish we were going on vacation, like you," I said. "It's gonna be really lonely with just Dad and me. Even with all the people at the parade."

Eunice stopped writing in her notebook for a second. And then her face lit up with a smile.

"Hold on, I have an idea. Why don't you take a break from homework to play with Oliver? I'll be right back."

I shrugged. "Okay."

After Eunice left, I looked underneath the desk, where Oliver the Maltese was sleeping. He was making cute little huffy-puffy sounds. I guess that's how dogs sound when they're snoring.

"Hey, Oliver," I said softly. "Do you want to play?"

Oliver's ears twitched, but he just kept snoring away.

I sighed. That was probably a no.

Instead I went back to my homework. We were doing long division, and it was pretty easy, although sometimes the teacher threw in things called remainders, to be tricky.

"I'll get you, remainders!" I muttered to myself

as I scribbled down my answers. Soon my paper was full of numbers.

Eunice finally came back into her room, and when she did, she was grinning from ear to ear.

"Come down to the kitchen, Mindy!" she said. "I have a surprise for you."

"A surprise?" I clapped with excitement. I love surprises!

Eunice's mom greeted us both with a big hug when we came into the kitchen.

"Mindy! You came just in time! I just finished making tteokguk."

"Tteokguk!" I exclaimed. "Really? But it isn't Lunar New Year yet!"

Tteokguk is a special soup with cute, oval-shaped pieces of rice cake that everyone in Korea eats during Lunar New Year. Mom used to make it every year, because eating the rice-cake soup is supposed to give you a fresh, clean start for the new year ahead.

I was wondering if I'd get to eat tteokguk this year, but I hadn't mentioned it to Dad. I didn't want to make him sad by reminding him of Mom.

"Eunice told me that you and your dad are going to stay in Florida for the holiday," said Mrs. Park. "So I wanted to give you a little taste of home. I'll pack some leftover soup for your dad so he can eat some when he gets off work too."

Eunice's mom is so nice! I gave her a big hug and sat down at the dining room table.

The soup was nice and hot, with strips of egg, beef, and dried seaweed arranged prettily in the bowl. It was so good! Almost as good as Mom's.

To make things even better, Oliver the Maltese came to sit next to me at the dining room table. The food smells must have woken him up! He stared at me with big puppy eyes, pretty much asking me to feed him.

I snuck him a few pieces of beef. He's lucky he's cute.

When we were done eating, Mrs. Park brought us plates full of cute, colorful rice cakes.

"Both Eunice and her dad really like rice cakes, so we always end up buying too many. Why don't

you take some to share with your classmates tomorrow? It's not like we can finish them all before we go to Seattle."

I thought back to the seaweed business I started several months ago. I guess sharing was okay as long as I didn't ask for anything back. My teacher, Mrs. Potts, said only trading snacks was banned, not just giving them!

"Okay, thank you!" I said with a big bow. Dad always said that I should bow to Korean adults in two different scenarios: one, if I was seeing them for the first time that day, and two, if they did something really nice for me.

Mrs. Park smiled. "No problem. Hope you and your dad enjoy the food."

I was feeling a bit better about Lunar New Year. Yummy food always makes everything better.

Chapter 3

Every Friday, my class does "What's New with You?" show-and-tell, where people who have exciting things going on can share with the class. When it was my turn, I showed everyone the plastic container of rice cakes that Mrs. Park had packed for me to bring to school.

My teacher, Mrs. Potts, frowned. "Mindy? What are those?"

"They're rice cakes!" I explained. "Tomorrow is Lunar New Year, so I wanted to share them with the class."

Priscilla, the girl who always sits in the front of class and asks everyone questions, raised her hand.

"Yes, Priscilla?" said Mrs. Potts, giving her a small nod.

"What is Lunar New Year?"

"That's a very good question." Mrs. Potts smiled at me. "Mindy, would you like to explain to the class about Lunar New Year?"

Oh boy. I tried to remember everything I'd learned about Lunar New Year in Korean school back in California.

"A long time ago in Asia, people used the moon to tell time instead of the sun. There's a whole separate calendar based on it," I began. "Some people still use the lunar calendar, and the New Year on that calendar is called Lunar New Year. People from all over Asia celebrate it! In China, Vietnam, and Korea, too! So Lunar New Year is New Year's Day but using the moon."

"That's so cool!" said Priscilla.

And then more hands shot up. There were so many that I couldn't possibly answer everyone's questions. I answered as many as I could before Mrs. Potts said, "All right, then. That was very educational. Thank you, Mindy. Are you going to share those rice cakes with everyone in the class?"

She gave me a look.

"Don't worry, Mrs. Potts, I'm not gonna try to trade them or anything. They're one hundred percent free!"

A few kids giggled. Operation Yummy Seaweed Business happened months ago, but people still know me as the seaweed-business girl.

Mrs. Potts laughed too. "All right, Mindy, if you say so. Would you like to go around and give everyone a rice cake?"

"Sure!"

I started walking around the class with the rice cakes and some napkins I'd brought from home. I first gave a rice cake to Mrs. Potts, because Dad says that I should always give things to adults first. It's Korean manners! She put it in her mouth and smiled.

"That's delicious, Mindy!" she said.

I gave her my biggest smile. I was so happy that Mrs. Potts liked the rice cake!

The first kid I gave a rice cake to was, of course, Sally, my best friend. She took a pink napkin from me and then used it to carefully grab one of the rice cakes.

"Thanks, Mindy!" she said.

But not everyone was that nice.

"Ew," said Melissa, one of Sally's friends. She wrinkled her nose. "Why is it so squishy? And what's in it?"

"Red bean! It's really sweet and yummy," I explained.

"*Beans?*" Melissa exclaimed. "Yuck! Get it away from me!"

A lot fewer people wanted to try the rice cakes after that.

But they didn't bother me much. They were missing out! It just meant there were more rice cakes for me and everyone else who actually liked them. The people who *did* like them *really* liked them and kept asking for more!

"Mindy, you have the best taste in snacks!" said Sally.

I beamed. Sally was so nice! What she said gave me an idea. I wasn't sure if it was going to work or not, but it was worth a try.

During recess, I asked Sally, "Hey, my dad and I are going to the Lunar New Year parade in Orlando tomorrow. Do you want to come with us? I heard it'll be really fun, and there's gonna be a lot of yummy snacks."

"Oh yeah!" Sally said. "I see ads about it every year. Sure! I have to ask my mom first, but I think I can go."

"Great!"

I was really excited. The parade would be much better with Sally by my side.

Lunar New Year just got a lot more fun.

Chapter 4

Dad was really happy that I asked Sally to come with us to the parade.

"That's great, Mindy!" he said as he tucked me into bed. "The more the merrier. I'm so glad that you and Sally are such good friends."

I hugged Mr. Shiba, my favorite Shiba Inu plush, close to my chest. "Do you have any friends who might want to come, Appa?" I asked.

He shrugged. "I don't really know my coworkers that well yet, and I'm not sure if they'd be interested in coming. I'm glad you were able to find someone to come with you, though!"

That made me sad. It had been several months

since we first moved to Florida, and it didn't look like Dad had any friends. I was glad that I at least had Sally.

"You should make friends with the people you work with," I said. "Bring them food! It worked for me."

Dad chuckled. "Okay, Mindy. I'll take that into consideration. Thanks for the advice."

"No problem."

After Dad went back downstairs, I pulled my blanket over my head. I'm not scared of the dark—not anymore, anyway. But sometimes it still gets really lonely. Plus, even though I was excited, I was still worried about tomorrow. What if the parade turned out to be really boring? I'd feel bad for dragging Sally along with me.

I reached down under my bed and got out Mr. Toe Beans, my soft corgi doll. I usually sleep with only one stuffed animal to show my dad that I'm all grown-up, but tonight called for *two*.

Sandwiched in between Mr. Shiba and Mr. Toe Beans, I drifted off to sleep.

That night, I dreamed that I was back in our apartment in California. Everything seemed normal, but no matter how much I looked, I couldn't find Mom or Dad! I ran outside to see if I could find them there, but I got lost in a big crowd of people.

It was a really scary dream!

"Mindy, wake up!"

When I opened my eyes, I saw Dad standing beside my bed. He was holding up Mr. Toe Beans with a concerned look on his face.

"Are you okay?" he said. "It sounded like you were having a nightmare. Mr. Toe Beans is here for a hug if you need one!"

I reached up and took Mr. Toe Beans from Dad. Usually, I didn't want Dad to see that I still liked hugging my stuffed animals, but today was a special occasion. My face still felt wet from the tears I cried during my nightmare, and even though the real Dad was right in front of me, I still felt really sad. I squeezed Mr. Toe Beans tightly.

"Thanks, Appa," I said.

"Do you want to talk about it?" Dad asked.

I shook my head. I was afraid that if I told Dad about my dream, it'd make him sad too.

"Okay, well. Why don't you go ahead and change out of your pajamas? We need to go pick up Sally soon."

Dad went back downstairs, and I sighed. Thanks to my nightmare, now I *really* didn't want to go to the parade, even with Sally coming along with us. It was a pretty bad start to the Lunar New Year.

I went to my closet and changed into my high-five T-shirt. Dad and I call it that because it's a cute periwinkle T-shirt with a golden-retriever puppy giving a tabby kitty a high five. It made me feel a bit better.

When I sat down at the dining room table to eat my toast and cereal, I asked, "Appa, what's the zodiac animal for this new year?

My favorite thing about the lunar calendar is the fact that every year has its own special animal from the Chinese zodiac. Last year's was a cute pig. But I didn't know what came after that.

Dad thought for a moment before replying, "Hmm, it's 2020, so it's the Year of the Rat!"

"Aw," I said. "Rats are so cute!"

I thought about Mr. Ratowski, the classroom pet rat that my old teacher had back in California. He was really small and cute, with his gray fur and black, beanlike eyes. Some people think rats are gross, but I don't think so at all. They just have a bad reputation!

"Hey, Mindy," Dad said suddenly. "Do you still fit into the hanbok that Mommy bought you last year? If you do, why don't you wear it to the parade since it's Lunar New Year? I know how much you love it."

A hanbok is a traditional Korean dress that people wear on holidays and special occasions. I wore my cute pink one last year, but I hadn't worn it ever since Mom died. Maybe it was time for me to bring it back out!

"That's a good idea, Appa!"

I ran up the stairs. I hoped that it'd still fit. My hanbok is really adorable, with pastel rainbow sleeves and a bright pink skirt. Mom and I spent a really long time in the hanbok store picking just the right one.

"Wait up!" Dad said. "Let me help you."

I rummaged through my closet until I found my hanbok. It was still wrapped in plastic so it wouldn't get dirty or wrinkled.

Dad helped me put it on. It was a little tighter and shorter than I remembered it being, but it still looked okay in my book!

"Hmm," Dad said. "Are you sure you're still comfortable in it? We'll have to get you a new one . . . somehow. I don't know if there are hanbok stores in Orlando, though."

"I can still wear it!" I said. "I don't care if it's a bit small."

Dad scratched his head. "If you're sure. I'm going to have to see if we can go up to Atlanta at some point later in the year so we can get you fitted for a new one."

I didn't want a new hanbok. The new one wouldn't be from Mom.

"This one is fine with me."

"Okay, I think it looks fine for now. Ready to go pick up Sally?"

"Yup!"

"All right." Dad smiled. "Let's go."

Chapter 5

When Sally got in the car, the first thing she did was tell me how pretty I looked in my hanbok.

"You look really nice!" she said. "Where did you get that dress?"

"It's a hanbok! And I got it in California," I said. "My mom bought it for me last year. It's a traditional dress that Korean people wear on special days like today."

"Cool!"

We headed straight for the parade in Orlando. While we were sitting in traffic, Sally took out a phone in a sky-blue case.

"Wow!" I said. "Is that your phone?"

"Yup! My mom bought it for me in case of emergencies, but I mainly just use it to play games. I'm not allowed to take it out at school, though. Wanna play?"

"Sure!"

Sally and I took turns playing a racing game that was super fun, even though Sally kept beating me by five hundred points.

"It's okay," said Sally. "You're really good for a beginner!"

When we were almost there, Sally put away her phone.

"I only have thirty percent battery left, so I'd better save it," she said.

We could hear the loud thumping of drums all the way from our car as we pulled into the parking lot. Everything else was drowned out by the loud chatter of the people outside.

"Wow, that sounds exciting!" said Sally.

Dad, Sally, and I got out of the car and walked toward the edge of the sidewalk, where we could get the best views of the parade.

Red Chinese lions danced with their mouths and eyes flapping open and closed, while long red and green dragons floated above everyone. People from many different parts of Asia came down the street wearing their traditional clothing. A lot of them smiled and waved at us as they passed, while others carried banners and flags.

I gave everyone a big smile as they walked by.

As I looked around at the other people watching the parade, I was glad that I wasn't the only one wearing traditional clothing. I didn't see anyone else wearing a hanbok, though!

"Hmm," Dad said. "Looks like there aren't any people representing Korea yet. The parade is still really interesting! Look over there at the taiko float, Mindy! Aren't those drums cool?"

Kids my age were walking down the street with taiko drums strapped across their chests. They were so good! The beat made me want to dance. Sally and I bounced up and down to the music.

It felt weird to see so many Asian people here. Even though there'd been a lot of Asian people back in California, here in Florida I'd only seen a few. In the last couple of months, I'd become used to being the only Asian kid in my school.

"This is so cool!" Sally exclaimed. "I never knew there were this many different Asian cultures."

"This isn't half of it!" I grinned. "We haven't even seen the Korean stuff!"

We saw more dancers, musicians, and other performers. And we kept waiting for the Korean group to come.

"I'm sure there will be someone representing Korea at some point," Dad said.

Finally, after the last performers went by, it was pretty clear that we weren't going to see any Korean performers today.

Last year, at the Lunar New Year festival in California, there was a group of samulnori people playing Korean drums, flutes, and gongs. There was also a K-pop performance, where lots of pretty girls danced onstage with their supercool moves! Dad said the performers were college students who were in samulnori and K-pop clubs in school, and I remember hoping I could be one of them someday.

But no matter how much I waited, I didn't hear any Korean flutes or gongs this year. Nor did I see anyone dancing to K-pop. It made me kind of sad that there wasn't anyone Korean in the parade, even though seeing Lunar New Year traditions from other Asian countries was pretty neat.

Dad must have seen the frown on my face, because he said, "It's okay, Mindy. We can have our own Lunar New Year celebration back at home after the festival. I think we still have our yutnori board somewhere."

That made me feel a little better. Yutnori is a fun Korean board game that my parents and I used to play every Lunar New Year. Maybe I could teach Sally how to play!

Suddenly, Sally tugged at my sleeve.

"Look, Mindy! It's Pikachu!"

I whirled around and saw a huge Pikachu balloon pass by us in the parade.

"Wow!" I said. "It's really Pikachu!"

"Hmm, I'm not sure how Pokémon is related to Lunar New Year," Dad said, sounding really confused. "Maybe they just have it for the little kids."

"Let's go take a picture with it!" Sally said. She pulled out her phone from her pocket and started running into the crowd, toward the balloon.

I turned to Dad. "Can we go take a picture with Pikachu, Appa?"

"Um, sure. But wait–"

I didn't hear what else my dad said, because I started running when he said "sure." I was too excited! Dad was much faster than me, so I was sure he was close behind.

Sally ran toward Pikachu and I tried my best to catch up. It was kind of hard to run in my hanbok, and I had to hold my skirt up so I wouldn't trip on it.

The Pikachu was moving slowly enough that we could keep pace with it while taking pictures.

"You go first, Mindy!" Sally said. "I'll take lots of good pictures with you and Pikachu."

I smiled really big and put up the peace sign as Sally took pictures of me.

"Cute!" said Sally. She sounded like one of the moms who come to volunteer for our class. "My turn!"

Sally handed me her phone, and I took pictures of her. She looked so happy! I hoped I looked happy in my pics too.

"That was fun, Appa!" I said. "I think we can go home now. . . ."

I trailed off when I realized that Dad wasn't behind me like I thought he was.

"Wait," I said slowly. "Where's my dad?"

"I'm not sure," replied Sally. "Wasn't he right behind us?"

We looked around, but Dad was nowhere in sight.

"Maybe he's still walking by Pikachu!" Sally suggested.

But by then, Pikachu had gone way ahead of us. And we couldn't find the balloon again because there were so many people around us. And there was still no Dad.

We were lost!

Chapter 6

No matter how much I looked, I couldn't find Dad. Everyone was laughing and having fun, but I just wanted to cry. It was almost exactly like my nightmare, but instead of being alone, at least I had Sally with me.

I held it together, but barely. I didn't want Sally to see me cry and be scared too.

"Let's hold hands so we don't get split up," Sally said. "It'd be really bad if we lost each other, too."

"Good idea." I tightly grabbed Sally's hand. It made me feel better that no matter what happened, at least we were in this together. "It's okay," I said. "I'm sure we'll be able to find my dad soon."

"Let's try going back where we came from," Sally said. "Maybe he just got lost in the crowd somewhere along the way."

Sally and I started walking in the opposite direction of the parade. But no matter how much we walked, we couldn't find Dad, even when we reached the beginning of the parade.

"Maybe we can't find him because he's walking around looking for us, too." I tried my best to not sound scared, but my voice still quivered. I really hoped we wouldn't be lost forever.

"Maybe we can call him?" Sally suggested. "You know your dad's number, right? You can use my phone!"

I looked down at my feet. "No, I don't. I knew his California one, but he got a new phone after we moved here, and I haven't memorized that one yet."

"Okay, then, we can call my mom! She can get us, and then your dad can just catch up with us later. No problem."

Sally got out her phone. But instead of dialing her mom's number, she glanced at her screen and looked at me with wide eyes. "Oh no. We're doomed!" she wailed.

"Why?" I said. "What's wrong?"

"My phone ran out of battery. It won't turn on!"

"It's okay!" I said, trying to remain hopeful. "We can just ask to borrow someone's phone."

Sally shook her head. "I don't know my mom's number either. She's just speed-dial one. This is really bad." She sniffed. "I really want my mom."

"It's okay!" I said again, tightening my grasp on Sally's hand. "My dad is still looking for us. If we look for him, and he looks for us, we're bound to run into each other, right?"

We walked and walked and walked, but Dad was nowhere to be seen. Eventually, the parade ended, and everyone in the audience moved toward the end of the street, where people were performing on a big stage.

My stomach growled. I had no idea how long Sally and I had walked around to find Dad, but I was really hungry! And scared. What if we were lost here forever? Did Dad know we were still here? I wanted to find Dad. And I wanted food!

"I'm hungry," I said. "Do you want to get something to eat?"

"Sure, do you have money?" asked Sally.

"Oh . . . no, I don't." I was so worried about being lost that I totally forgot that you needed money to pay for food! Dad always bought food for the two of us, so I never carried money with me. My heart started beating really fast. Sally was right. We were doomed!

I was about to cry when Sally said, "It's okay! I have an emergency twenty-dollar bill in my phone case. You can pay me back later!"

Sally fished the money out of her case. She was a true hero!

"I don't know if twenty dollars is enough for both lunch and dinner, though," Sally said with a frown. "Maybe we can share something now and get something else later!"

She looked worried, and I bit my lip. I really hoped we could find Dad soon!

"Don't worry," I said, even though I was scared

too. "My dad would never leave us here. Maybe he just got hungry and stopped to eat something!"

Sally looked kind of doubtful, but she didn't say anything.

Together, we wandered over to the food stalls. There were so many options, but only a few were "within our budget." Sally explained that her mom says "within our budget" all the time during important business calls with her company. "It means that we have enough money for something!" she said excitedly. But then Sally's bottom lip began quivering. "What if I never see my mom again?"

I almost started crying too, when I heard Dad's voice.

"Mindy! Sally!"

I spun around. It was really Dad!

"Appa!" I yelled.

Dad ran to me and picked me up, squeezing me into a tight hug before snuggling his face against mine. His face was wet, like he'd been crying for a really long time. Seeing Dad cry finally made me cry too.

"It's okay, Dad," I said. "You found us! I'm safe."

"So, you were right about them being where the food is!" a lady said then.

I looked past Dad's shoulder to see a pretty Asian lady with short black hair. She looked happy to see me, even though I had no idea who she was.

"We were walking all over the place to find you . . . but then we got hungry," I said to Dad sheepishly.

He laughed and then smiled at both Sally and me. "Well, I'm glad we found you two in the end. You scared me!"

"Sorry we ran off," I apologized. "Being lost was really scary, so I promise I won't do that again."

"I'm sorry too," said Sally. "I was the one who ran after Pikachu first."

Dad patted both our shoulders. "It's okay, girls. I think we all learned a very important lesson today. Thanks for the apology, though."

"I tried to call you, but I forgot your number," I said.

"And my phone ran out of battery, so I couldn't call my mom," added Sally.

"Oh dear," Dad said. "Let's make sure you girls know all the important numbers when we get home. And next time, when you get lost, be sure to stay in one place so you're easier to find."

"Okay, Appa," I replied.

He then let go of me to gesture at the lady still standing behind him.

"Mindy, Sally, I want you to meet Julie. She's one of my coworkers, and I happened to run into her while searching for you girls. I kind of . . . panicked when I couldn't find you two, and she helped calm me down."

Julie waved him off. "It was nothing," she said. "Your dad looked like he needed help, so I helped! Anyone would have done it." She then waved at us with a big smile. "Hi, Mindy. Hi, Sally. It's so nice to meet both of you. I'm glad you two are safe."

I shook Julie's hand. "Pleased to make your acquaintance," I said, like they did in the old black-and-white movies I used to watch with Mom.

Dad coughed, and a mysterious look appeared on his face. "Well, Julie, if you don't have anything else to do, we'd love it if you'd join us for the rest of the festival."

"We would?" I asked.

Daddy shot me a nervous glance, like I'd said something I shouldn't have. He laughed, but instead of his usual booming laugh, his voice sounded weird and squeaky.

"Of course we would, Mindy! Don't be silly. Maybe we can all go grab lunch together? With the girls in very close proximity, of course."

Dad was acting very strange. I was about to ask him what was wrong when a man on the stage behind the food stalls announced, "Welcome to the Lunar New Year festival! We hope you enjoyed the parade. It's always so nice to see the traditions and festivities of the many different cultures we have here in Orlando. But don't leave yet! We have a lot of performances lined up for you here onstage today while you enjoy the delicious food. You're all in for a treat!"

"Quick," Dad said, gently pushing me toward a food-truck line. "Let's go get food now so we don't miss the show!"

"Okay," I said, narrowing my eyes. He wasn't off the hook yet!

Chapter 7

We ended up getting some yummy egg rolls and dumplings. Being lost definitely made me super hungry! But I still wanted to have our usual Korean New Year food too, so I mentioned it to Dad.

"Let's stop by the Korean supermarket on our way home and buy lots of our favorite food there!" he suggested.

It was the best idea I'd heard all day.

Carefully holding our paper plates of food, we walked around until we found enough seats for all four of us. It was really hard to find empty seats. By the time we sat down, our food had all cooled down.

"Wow," Dad said. "I can see why they had to move locations. This is a popular event!"

Compared to the Asian food in California, the food was just okay, especially since it was now cold. But the performances onstage were still pretty fun! There was a great group from Vietnam, who came out with parasols and danced. Then a couple of Chinese ladies danced with long, colorful ribbons. Every performance was so good!

Since there weren't any Korean floats or groups in the parade, I really hoped there would be someone performing onstage. I was just about to give up when I heard one of my favorite K-pop songs blasting from the speakers.

"This is it!" I yelled. "Finally, a Korean performance!"

I glanced at Sally to make sure she was paying attention to the stage. She was. I was so happy to show her something Korean, even though K-pop isn't *exactly* a New Year tradition!

After a few minutes, a group of five girls came

onto the stage. But there was something weird about the group.

Sally squinted her eyes. "Wait . . . is it just me, or . . . are none of the girls in that group Asian?"

"No, there's one Asian girl in the back," Julie said. "But you're right, Sally. Besides her, no one else is Asian."

"Hmm," Dad said. "I guess this is just a K-pop appreciation group. Maybe they're just trying to show how popular Korean music is?"

I didn't know how to feel about the group. They were really pretty and danced great! But I was still sad that during this entire day, we hadn't seen a single Korean person in the parade or festival.

I missed California.

Dad must have noticed that I was sad, because at the end of the last performance, he squeezed my shoulder and said, "Why don't we go back home and have our own super-awesome *Korean* New Year celebration?"

He turned to Julie and Sally. "And we'd be happy for you both to come, if you can? We can stop at the

46

Korean market first to pick up what we need."

Sally grinned. "Sure! I'm excited to try some yummy Korean food!"

I wanted to give Sally a big hug. I was so happy she could come over!

"Sounds like fun!" said Julie. "And yeah, if it's really okay with you, Brian, I'd be happy to join."

My jaw dropped. Julie was coming over to our house! Did this mean Julie and Dad were . . . *friends*? I got really excited. Finally, Dad was friends with one of his coworkers!

"Great!" Instead of saying "great" normally, Dad yelled so loudly that the lady in front of us turned to glare at us.

"Oops, sorry," said Dad. His face was getting a little red. He was acting so strange today!

Julie laughed and said, "Okay, well, text me your address and I'll meet you guys there after we go to the market."

While Dad was sending her our address, Sally tugged at my sleeve. She wiggled her eyebrows at me.

"Why are you acting so weird?" I whispered to Sally when Julie and Dad weren't looking.

"Mindy, I think your dad has a crush on Julie. And I think Julie likes him back!"

"But how?" I asked. "They barely know each other!"

Sally shrugged. "Adults are weird. Plus, they're coworkers, right? So they aren't *total* strangers!"

I didn't know how to feel about what Sally said. But I knew she was definitely onto something. I'd never seen Dad act that way around another person. He wasn't even that nervous around my mom!

Adults really confuse me sometimes.

Chapter 8

On our way to the Korean supermarket, I asked Sally, "Hey, did you know that in Korea, we're nine years old?"

Sally wrinkled her nose. "What? How?"

"In Korea, you're already one year old when you're born. And then you age up whenever it's the New Year!"

"Whoa," she said. "That's pretty cool! Although I wouldn't want to be older than I am now."

I couldn't believe what she said. "What, really? How come?"

"The older you get, the closer you get to becoming a grown-up! And then you have to do

49

scary things like pay bills and taxes! My mom told me that being an adult is the worst. And it looks bad too! She's always really busy and stressed."

"Well, I wouldn't say it's the worst," Dad said from the front. "You girls have a lot of fun things to look forward to. But it *can* be pretty challenging sometimes!"

Finally Dad found a parking spot. He barely had the car turned off when I flung open the door. I was ready to shop for all the food I'd missed out on today!

"Come on!" I said to Sally. "Let's go look at the snacks!"

"Mindy!" Dad said. "Can you please stay in the car until I get out? I already lost you and Sally once today. I don't want to do that again."

"Okay," I said, slumping down in the seat. I didn't want to wait, but I did anyway. I still felt bad for giving Dad a hard time earlier today.

In the end, we had to wait for Julie to park her car too. We all met at the front of the supermarket before we went in. There were so many people in the store that some of the lines were spilling out into the parking lot!

"Here's the game plan," Dad said. "We should all stick together, but just in case we get separated in the crowd, Sally should stick with me and Mindy should stick with Julie so each group has someone who knows what to look for. We need rice cakes, stir-fried glass noodles, and honey pastries, okay? And ingredients for jeon, Korean pancakes! Mindy, do you know what everything looks like?"

"Yup!"

"Okay, then, let's go!"

We went through the doors. Crowds of people filled the store, and loud, happy music was blasting from the speakers. Everyone was yelling and waving their hands in the air, trying to reach the products on sale. A lot of the food was already sold out!

"Quick!" I yelled. "Grab the rice cakes! And the honey pastries!"

"Excuse me! Excuse me!" Dad yelled as he pushed the cart around in the store. There were so many people, and Dad was too nice to push past them. Sometimes he even let other people push *him*!

"I have a better idea," said Julie, loud enough that all of us could hear. "How about Mindy and I go farther into the store to get everything we need in those sections? Brian, you can stay here with Sally and the cart."

"That's an excellent idea!" I said. "Now can we please go get the food?"

I didn't want any of the food to run out!

"Sure," Dad said. "I'll pick up a few things near the front of the store with Sally while you two do that. Let's meet at the cash register."

"Got it," said Julie.

Unlike Dad, Julie wasn't afraid to push past people. She wasn't mean and didn't hurt anybody, but she moved way faster and found everything we needed to find, plus a few more yummy things like dumplings and shrimp crackers. I liked Julie already!

By the time we were done, our cart was full of

snacks, rice cakes, sweet rice crackers, and stir-fried glass noodles.

It was finally starting to feel like a Korean New Year!

Chapter 9

When we got home, Dad got out our board and game pieces for yutnori, my favorite Korean game! It's a traditional racing game that people play on Lunar New Year. And before Mom got sick, my parents and I played it every year.

Last year, Mom, Dad, and I played against one another, but today, Dad said, "Since we have an even number of people, why don't we do teams? Sally and Mindy, you guys can be in one team while Julie and I can be in the other."

"But Dad, I want to be on a team with you!" I complained.

I was a little mad. Sally was my best friend.

But whenever we played games with our family or friends, Dad was always on my team. Why did Dad want to be on a team with Julie?

"But then who will I be on a team with?" Sally asked, sounding confused.

She had a point. Since Sally was my friend, I guess it made sense that she'd be my partner.

"Okay," I agreed. "Sally and I can be a team."

In the first few minutes, Dad and I taught Sally and Julie how to play. The game is pretty simple, since you just toss four sticks and move your piece on the board depending on how many sticks land faceup. If all of them land either faceup or facedown, it's super lucky and you can throw again!

"It's also really good if you land on one of the corners," I told Sally as the four of us sat down around the board. "Then you can cut across diagonally to the finish line!"

"Okay, got it," Sally said.

I didn't want Dad to win. First of all, I like to win! And second, I was still kind of mad at him for wanting to be on Julie's team.

Dad eyed the clock. "Usually, you're supposed to do two to four rounds, but I think we only have time for one round since we should start preparing for dinner soon. That sound good to everyone?"

Sally shrugged, and I said, "Yes!"

It was going to be a lightning round, all or nothing. I was so excited!

"Let's win for sure!" I told Sally, holding my hand up for a high five.

"Yes!" she said. "Let's!"

She gave me a high five.

I told Sally she could throw first. She threw the sticks, and they landed all faceup!

"Woo-hoo!" I cheered. "That was awesome. Throw again!"

This time the sticks landed with two of them faceup.

"Okay, so four from the first throw and two from the second," I said. "Move six places. That was a really good throw!"

Sally beamed and moved our piece forward

six times. We were doing so well already!

Dad rolled next. He got three sticks faceup.

"Oops," he said. "Sorry."

Julie smiled. "That's okay. It's only the first throw."

"Ha-ha!" I said as I picked up the sticks. "Now our team will win for sure!"

I threw the sticks.

They landed with only *one* stick faceup!

"Noooo!" I yelled. "This can't be!"

Dad chuckled. "That's too bad, Mindy. Maybe you'll throw better next time!"

Julie was next. She tossed the sticks and all of them landed facedown! All sticks facedown meant she could move *five* places, *and* she got to throw again! The second time, she threw the sticks and got two faceup. She moved her and Dad's piece seven times, and it ended up on one of the corners!

This was really bad. Now Dad and Julie had a direct path to the finish line. They were only six places away from winning!

"It's okay!" I said. "We can still win!"

I didn't want Sally to feel discouraged while she went.

She threw her sticks. This time she got three sticks faceup.

"Aw," she said. "Sorry for the bad throw."

"No, this is good!" I said. "Look where our game piece ended up!"

Thanks to Sally's throw, our game piece reached the same corner as Dad's and Julie's!

Game. On.

"No!" Dad yelled, like I had a couple of minutes ago. "You got us!"

"Wait," Sally said. "What's going on?"

"If you land on the same space as the enemy team, you can kick them out of the space and they have to go all the way back to the beginning!" I explained. "And then you can go again."

"Wow, that's so mean!" Sally said as she threw the sticks again. But she was smiling like I was. There's a reason why Sally and I are friends. "Sorry, Julie and Mr. Kim."

"That's quite all right, Sally," Dad said as he moved his piece back to the starting line. "That was a very lucky throw."

Sally's throw got us only two spaces this time, but it was way better than having to go back to the beginning. "Good job!" I said as she moved our piece.

It was Dad's turn, and this time, all his sticks landed facedown.

"Yes!" exclaimed Julie. "Way to go, Brian!"

Dad threw the sticks again. Three landed faceup. They had almost caught up to us already!

It was my turn to throw now. I was still really embarrassed that I got only one stick faceup the last time I went. But hopefully this time would be better.

"You can do it, Mindy!" Sally cheered. "Let's win this game!"

I stuck out the hand clutching the sticks in Sally's direction. "Let's do a lucky handshake!"

"Okay!" Sally's hand clasped mine so the sticks were sandwiched in between us. "Good luck!"

I then threw the sticks, and they all landed faceup! I threw again. Two were faceup. That was more than enough for us to win!

I moved our piece to the finish line and jumped up and down with Sally.

"YESSSSS!"

We won!

Chapter 10

After we cleaned up the game pieces, we went into the kitchen to prepare yummy food for our Lunar New Year feast.

"I just have to fry some kimchi, zucchini, and cod to make the jeon, and then we'll be all set!" Dad said.

Jeon are like pancakes, Korean-style. You mix all the ingredients into a batter and cook them in a pan like you do with American pancakes.

"Do you want me to help?" Julie asked. "I'm good with a knife and cutting board."

"I can help too!" I said. "What can I do, Appa?"

Dad nervously glanced back and forth between Julie and me.

"Well, Mindy, you can't help cut things or fry stuff in the pan," he said. "But you and Sally can be in charge of covering everything with flour after Julie's done chopping up all the ingredients! And then I can fry the jeon in the pan."

"Sounds good!"

We washed our hands, and then it was time for some food magic!

Just like she said, Julie was really good at cutting everything into thin slices. She was way better than Dad, who still accidentally hurts himself while cooking sometimes. He's the reason we have so many Band-Aids around the house, not me!

In almost no time at all, Julie had everything laid out neatly in a big plate, and Dad seasoned everything with some salt and pepper.

"Okay," said Dad after he took out the bag of flour. "Now what we're going to do is cover everything with flour. You have to make sure to get both sides of everything. I hope you don't mind getting your hands dirty, Sally, because this can get kind of messy!"

"I don't mind." Sally smiled. "It sounds like a lot of fun!"

Dad brought out the small pink aprons that I like to wear when I help Dad out in the kitchen.

"You girls can wear these. Sally, I don't want your mom to get mad at me because you have flour all over you."

Sally giggled. "Thanks, Mr. Kim."

Sally and I put on our aprons and started covering all the food with flour. I was afraid it might get boring, but with Sally by my side, it was actually fun! We laughed and joked around as we covered the zucchini, kimchi, and cod. We were done in no time, and Dad took out some eggs from the fridge and beat them in a bowl.

"Anything else I can do to help?" Julie asked.

Dad glanced around nervously again before saying, "You can help reheat the other things we got from the store while I make the jeon."

"Sure!"

Sally and I watched Dad as he took the flour-covered food and dipped it in egg before frying it in the pan. There was a cool sizzling sound whenever the food hit the pan, but after a while it got boring. So we helped Julie reheat the food in the microwave instead.

Soon the entire house was filled with the yummy smell of jeon, bulgogi, dumplings, and stir-fried glass noodles. It was a whole feast!

While we were eating, Julie, Dad, and I shared stories about the different things we did for Lunar New Year. Julie said that back home in New York, her family always gathered around and made dumplings. They also ate lots of fish and exchanged red envelopes that had money inside them.

Dad looked at me. "We don't do red envelopes like Chinese people do, but we *do* give New Year's money. That reminds me, Mindy. Do you want to do sebae after we finish eating?"

"What's sebae?" Sally asked.

"It's when I bow to Dad and wish him happy new year, and then he gives me some money!" I said. "Usually you bow to your grandparents, but my grandparents live far away from us, so I just bow to my dad instead. It's what people do for Lunar New Year in Korea."

"Wow!" said Sally. "How come we don't have traditions like that in America?"

"Beats me." I shrugged. "But if you bow to my dad, I'm sure he'll give you money too. Right, Dad?"

"Mindy!" Dad exclaimed.

Oops. I guess I shouldn't have said that!

Dad sighed. "Sebae isn't just about the money. Yes, a little pocket change is nice, but it's meant to be a way for your elders to bless you for the new year."

Julie laughed. "I can give some money too," she said. "Maybe I can give some to Sally, and you can give some to Mindy?"

"You don't have to," said Dad.

"Don't sweat it. It'd be my pleasure!" Julie said. "I just wish I had red envelopes!"

Dad got out comfy cushions and put them on the living room floor. He and Julie sat facing Sally and me.

"First, I want to make sure you two know why

we do sebae, because, like I said before, it's not just about getting money," said Dad, shooting me a look. "In Korea, respect for your elders is very important. So, in order to *earn* your money, you have to wish the adults a happy and healthy new year while you give them a deep bow. And the adults bless you, too. Sally, Mindy can show you how to bow."

"Yup!" I said. "I learned how at Korean school last year."

"Okay," said Sally. "Show me how!"

I went to stand right in front of Dad. He gave me a big smile.

"Well," I said. "First you put your hands clasped in front of your head like this, right hand over left." I lifted my hands so they were both at the level of my eyes. "Then slowly sit down, putting your left knee to the floor, and then the right."

Being careful to not trip on my dress, I knelt down onto the floor.

"And finally, bend forward so you're halfway to the floor before you stand up again."

I did my bow to show Sally.

"Wow," Sally said after I stood back up. "That looks hard."

"It's really easy!" I promised. "We can do it together!"

Step by step, I guided Sally into a proper jeol.

When we were done, I looked up to see that Dad was taking pictures of both Sally and me. He looked really proud, and Julie smiled at us too.

"You two were so great!" Dad said. "Happy Lunar New Year. Hope you both have a great rest of the school year! Study hard but don't forget to have fun, okay?"

"Okay!" we said.

After, Sally and I each got a twenty-dollar bill! Now we were a bit richer!

Chapter

11

Soon it was time for Sally to go back home.

"Thanks for having me!" Sally said. "It was really fun! Well, except the getting lost part."

Dad frowned. "Right. I'm so sorry that happened, Sally."

"Don't worry, Mr. Kim," said Sally. "It was my fault anyway. Mindy and I were the ones who ran off after the Pikachu balloon! My mom will understand, I think. And I'll make sure to memorize her number!"

Her mom drove up to the front of our house, and Sally gave me a hug before she left.

"See you at school!" she said.

"Yeah, see you!"

After Sally was gone, it was time to say goodbye to Julie.

"Thank you so much for having me over," Julie said warmly. "I was bracing myself for spending this holiday alone, but in the end, I'm really glad that I didn't."

"We were glad to have you over as well," said Dad. "Mindy and I don't really know that many people in the area either, so it was great to see you."

Although I still didn't know how to feel about Julie, she *was* pretty nice, and we'd had a lot of fun together today. And I liked that she made Dad happy.

"Yeah," I said. "Don't be a stranger!"

Julie looked really happy, like Dad and I had just given her a puppy.

"See you at work, Brian," she said to my dad as we walked her out to her car. "And I'll see you around, Mindy?"

She gave me a big smile.

"Yup!" I grinned.

After Julie left, Dad and I went back into the house. What a day it had been! I wasn't sure if I could still love the holiday as much without Mom here to celebrate with us, but maybe I could still like it. And we could have new traditions and make new memories with our new friends.

Once I was back upstairs, I showered and put on my pink corgi pajamas. Even though the hanbok was pretty, it felt good to wear comfier clothes again.

Dad came to my room to tuck me into bed.

"Wow," he said. "We had a really busy day today."

"Yup," I said. "I hope the next Lunar New Year is more boring."

Dad laughed. "You and me both, kid."

He was about to leave when I said, "Appa?"

"Yes?"

"Do you like Julie?"

Dad's face turned strawberry red. "Why do you say that?"

"So, you *do* like her!" I said. "Sally said you did, and I guess she was right."

"Well," Dad said. "It's too early to tell. But she *is* very kind. We usually don't really interact with each other much at work, but today she helped me a lot when you girls went missing. Are you uncomfortable with the fact that I might like her, Mindy?"

I shrugged. I was a little sad because I missed Mom, but I knew Dad couldn't miss her and be sad forever. I don't think Mom would want that, either.

"I just hope she makes you happy."

Dad smiled, but his eyes were shiny, like he was about to cry.

"Aw, thanks, Mindy."

He gave me a little kiss on the forehead.

"But you have to tell me before you marry her, okay!" I yelled, jabbing a finger into Dad's chest. "And get my permission!"

Dad jumped in surprise. "Mindy! It's *way* too early for that. But sure, if that ever happens, with Julie or any other person, I will definitely let you know."

"Good," I said with a firm nod. "Good night, Appa."

"Good night, Mindy."

Dad turned off the light, and I moved Mr. Toe Beans back under my bed. I still had Mr. Shiba with me. One was enough for me tonight.

Even though it wasn't my birthday, I did feel older than I had before Lunar New Year. Today wasn't perfect, but it was definitely better than I thought it would be.

"Happy Lunar New Year, Mr. Shiba," I whispered to Mr. Shiba. "Congrats, you're now officially two years old."

Mr. Shiba, of course, didn't say anything. But he did look kind of happy.

I was happy too, as I closed my eyes. Even though I'd had a scary nightmare last night, I was sure I'd have a really fun dream tonight, filled with food, friends, and happy celebrations.

I was so excited to sleep! And I was even more excited for the Lunar New Year ahead.

Acknowledgments

When I first set out to plan this series, I knew right away that I wanted to write a book about the fun Korean traditions that my parents kept alive in our family despite the fact that we moved to the United States more than twenty years ago. Aside from the phone calls and infrequent visits back home, our traditions were the only way to keep connected to our roots. For that reason, I would like to thank my parents for never letting me feel any less Korean and doing their best to keep traditions alive in our family. 사랑해요.

I'd also like to thank my agent, Penny Moore, and my editor, Alyson Heller, who are always so enthusiastic about Mindy and her adventures.

Thank you also to Dung Ho, my illustrator, who never fails to draw such gorgeous and fun art for Mindy that Kid Me would have loved so much. You bring Mindy to life in ways I could have never imagined.

My friends, of course, were also vital to my writing process. Writing is often a lonely experience, and I'm so lucky to not have to go about this life alone. Thank you, as always, to Aneeqah Naeem, who is sitting across from me as I write this sentence. Our writing dates feed my soul. Thank you also to Katie Zhao, Amelie Zhao, Rey Noble, Faridah Abike-Iyimide, Sharon Choi, Francesca Flores, Annie Lee, Chelsea Chang, Shiyun Sun, Luke Chou, Anita Chen, Brianna Lei, Bernice Yau, Kaiti Liu, Angelica Tran, Oanh Le, Victor Hu, Eunji Lee, and all my other friends who make my life brighter every day.

I'm also so grateful for everyone who reached out and told me how excited they are to meet Mindy. Thank you especially to the teachers who have said they'll incorporate the Mindy Kim books, as well as other diverse literature, into their classrooms. You are changing so many lives, and we're all so lucky to have you.

Last but not least, thank you so much to you, reader! Thank you for joining Mindy as she goes on her adventures. I'm sure she's glad to have a friend like you by her side.

Don't miss Mindy's next adventure!

About the Author

Lyla Lee is the author of the Mindy Kim series as well as the upcoming YA novel *I'll Be the One*. Although she was born in a small town in South Korea, she's since then lived in various parts of the United States, including California, Florida, and Texas. Inspired by her English teacher, she started writing her own stories in fourth grade and finished her first novel at the age of fourteen. After working various jobs in Hollywood and studying psychology and cinematic arts at the University of Southern California, she now lives in Dallas, Texas. When she is not writing, she is teaching kids, petting cute dogs, and searching for the perfect bowl of shaved ice. You can visit her online at lylaleebooks.com.

Solve each problem with the smartest third-grade inventor!

EBOOK EDITIONS ALSO AVAILABLE

Aladdin

simonandschuster.com/kids

Looking for another great book?
Find it
IN THE MIDDLE.

Fun, fantastic books for kids
in the in-be**TWEEN** age.

IntheMiddleBooks.com

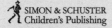 SIMON & SCHUSTER
Children's Publishing   /SimonKids   @SimonKids

Mindy Kim and the
Yummy Seaweed Business

Don't miss more fun adventures
with **Mindy Kim**!

BOOK 2:
Mindy Kim and the Lunar New Year Parade

Coming soon:

BOOK 3:
Mindy Kim and the Birthday Puppy

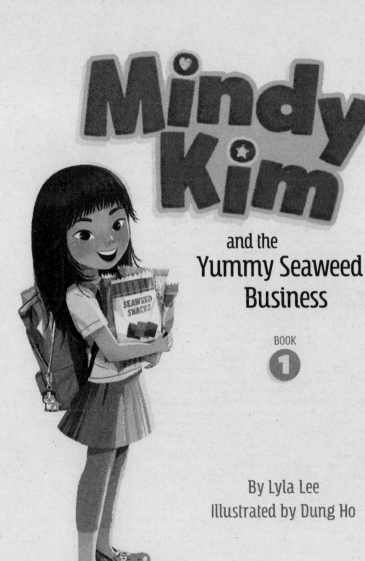

Mindy Kim

and the
Yummy Seaweed
Business

BOOK
1

By Lyla Lee
Illustrated by Dung Ho

ALADDIN
New York London Toronto Sydney New Delhi

If you purchased this book without a cover, you should be aware that this book is stolen property. It was reported as "unsold and destroyed" to the publisher, and neither the author nor the publisher has received any payment for this "stripped book."

This book is a work of fiction. Any references to historical events, real people, or real places are used fictitiously. Other names, characters, places, and events are products of the author's imagination, and any resemblance to actual events or places or persons, living or dead, is entirely coincidental.

ALADDIN

An imprint of Simon & Schuster Children's Publishing Division

1230 Avenue of the Americas, New York, New York 10020

First Aladdin paperback edition January 2020

Text copyright © 2020 by Lyla Lee

Illustrations copyright © 2020 by Dung Ho

Also available in an Aladdin hardcover edition.

All rights reserved, including the right of reproduction in whole or in part in any form.

ALADDIN and related logo are registered trademarks of Simon & Schuster, Inc.

For information about special discounts for bulk purchases, please contact Simon & Schuster Special Sales at 1-866-506-1949 or business@simonandschuster.com.

The Simon & Schuster Speakers Bureau can bring authors to your live event. For more information or to book an event contact the Simon & Schuster Speakers Bureau at 1-866-248-3049 or visit our website at www.simonspeakers.com.

Book designed by Laura Lyn DiSiena

The illustrations for this book were rendered digitally.

The text of this book was set in Haboro.

Manufactured in the United States of America 0320 OFF

10 9 8 7 6 5 4 3 2

Library of Congress Cataloging-in-Publication Data

Names: Lee, Lyla, author. | Ho, Dung, illustrator.

Title: Mindy Kim and the yummy seaweed business / by Lyla Lee ; illustrated by Dung Ho.

Description: New York : Aladdin, 2020. | Series: Mindy Kim ; 1 | Audience: Ages 6-9 |

Summary: Mindy Kim wants to fit in at her new school, but her favorite lunch leads to scorn, then a thriving business, and finally big trouble.

Identifiers: LCCN 2019026740 (print) | LCCN 2019026741 (eBook) |

ISBN 9781534440074 (paperback) | ISBN 9781534440098 (hardcover) |

ISBN 9781534440081 (eBook)

Subjects: CYAC: Moving, Household–Fiction. | Schools–Fiction. | Korean Americans–Fiction. | Single-parent families–Fiction. | Grief–Fiction.

Classification: LCC PZ7.1.L419 Min 2020 (print) | LCC PZ7.1.L419 (eBook) | DDC [Fic]–dc23

LC record available at https://lccn.loc.gov/2019026740

LC eBook record available at https://lccn.loc.gov/2019026741

For all the new kids out there. You're not alone.

Chapter 1

My name is Mindy Kim.

I'm seven and a half years old. That's old enough to ride a bike around our street, but not old enough to have my own puppy—or at least that's what my dad said.

I don't really agree with him, but our old apartment in California wasn't big enough for a puppy anyway. I looked it up, and the experts on the Internet say that puppies need lots of room to run outdoors.

Now that we've moved into a house with a big backyard, we can really get a puppy! I just have to convince my dad that it's a good idea first.

So far, no such luck. Dad wants me to prove that I can be "responsible" enough for a puppy first . . . and then he'll "consider" getting me one.

I decorated my own room to show Dad I'm "responsible." I'm trying to be more grown-up, so I only put three dog stuffed animals on my bed. There are ten more under my bed, but Dad doesn't need to know that. They'll just have to take turns.

After I finished, I was looking through a website on huskies, one of my *favorite* kinds of dogs, when I heard Dad say, "Mindy? Can you help me with these boxes?"

CRASH!

"Dad!" I ran downstairs to see him standing over a box of broken dishes.

"Oh no!" he said. "These were your mom's favorites."

He looked so sad, like he was about to cry. I wished I'd brought one of my stuffed dogs with me. I'd even let him hug Snowball, my favorite white husky.

I miss Mom, but I know Dad misses her a lot

more. She died a few months ago because she was really sick for a long time.

"It's okay," I said. "It was an accident. Mom wouldn't be mad."

Dad smiled. "No, she wouldn't. She was nice like that."

Dad and I finished unpacking and cleaning up the kitchen. The kitchen in our apartment in California was way smaller, so our things only filled up half the cabinets in our new house.

When we were done, Dad ordered pizza. He remembered to ask for pineapples on top, just the way I like it.

We waited for the pizza in our new dining room. Sitting at the table felt weird. All our stuff looked strange and small in this new, big house.

"Dad?" I asked. "Why did we never live in a house like this in California?"

"Everything is a lot cheaper in Florida than in California," Dad explained. "Plus, I got a big raise for transferring out here."

The pizza finally came. And it smelled so good

that my mouth watered before we even opened the box.

Dad handed me the largest slice.

"So, are you excited for school on Monday?" he asked.

The pizza dropped from my hands and right onto the floor. Oops.

Dad cringed. There was a large greasy, pizza-shaped stain on our new rug. "It's okay, honey. You eat, and I'll clean this up."

But I wasn't hungry anymore. Dad mentioning school had made me lose my appetite. Monday was only two days away. I'd never gone to a new school before. I didn't even know what the kids here would be like! And what if the teachers were mean?

I liked my friends and teachers in California. I wished we could just go back.

Dad returned with some cleaning supplies and frowned when he saw that I wasn't eating any of the pizza.

"Mindy," he said, "this move is going to be better for both of us! We could both use a fresh start."

Then I got a brilliant idea.

"Appa?" I said in my most innocent voice, using the Korean word for "Daddy." "Do you know what would *really* help us have a fresh start?"

Dad shook his head. "I already know what you are going to say. And we can't get a dog right now. You and I have to get settled in first."

Well, dog poop. He read my mind. It was worth a shot.

I was still pouting when Dad picked up the pizza box.

"Do you really not want any of the pizza? I guess I'll just have to finish it all by myself. . . ."

"No!"

I grabbed a slice before Dad could walk away. He smiled and put the pizza back on the table.

"Thanks for the pizza," I said. "But I'm still not looking forward to school."

"I know, sweetie, I know," said Dad. "But can you at least try? Maybe it won't be as bad as you think."

I hoped he was right.

Chapter 2

The more I thought about going to school, the more nervous I was. I couldn't even sleep! By Monday morning I had decided I just wasn't going to go.

"I don't want to go to school!" I yelled, and slammed the door of my room.

"You have to, sweetie," Dad said. "It's the first day! Why don't you give it a chance? You'll be lost if you don't go today!"

I groaned but came back out.

Dad was right. Moving to a new neighborhood on the other side of the country was confusing enough. The last thing I needed was to be even more confused.

"Okay, fine," I said. "But I get to eat ice cream when I come back."

"I'll have a bowl of mint chocolate chip ice cream waiting for you on the dinner table," promised Dad. "With chocolate syrup and sprinkles! Just the way you like it."

I sat in the back seat and didn't say anything the entire way to school.

Dad made funny faces in the mirror.

I didn't smile.

He told a funny joke.

I didn't laugh.

He said, "Look, Mindy! A cute dog!"

It was hard, but I didn't look.

I was too mad at Dad for making me go to a new school. For moving me here. Even though I knew why we moved here, that didn't mean I felt any better about it.

We finally arrived at Wishbone Elementary School. It was pretty for a school, and right by the beach too. But it wasn't enough. It didn't have Diya, one of my best friends. And it didn't have the big hills that we could roll down during recess.

I watched as the other kids got off the school buses. My old school had kids of many different colors. But here, no one looked like me.

I was almost out of the car when Dad said, "Don't forget your lunch!"

The only thing that was the same was my lunch. Dad had packed me the same rice, kimchi, rolled eggs, and dried seaweed snacks that I had eaten for lunch in California.

Lunch was my favorite subject already.

Chapter 3

My new teacher's name is Mrs. Potts. It's easy to remember, because it's just "pots" with another *t*. I asked Dad if I could ask her where the extra *t* came from, but he said it would be rude.

"Welcome!" said Mrs. Potts when I walked into the classroom. "You must be . . . Min-jung." She frowned as she tried to say my Korean name. "Do you have an English name?"

"I go by Mindy," I told her, like Dad told me to do.

"Oh, Mindy! What a pretty name!" Mrs. Potts smiled. "Have a seat wherever you want."

I didn't like Mrs. Potts. I missed Ms. Lin, my old

teacher in California. Ms. Lin said my Korean name was pretty too.

The only empty seat was by a girl with blond pigtails and pink glasses. She was so pretty! It was hard not to stare.

"Hi!" she said when I sat down in my seat. "My name is Sally. What is your name?"

"Mindy," I said. "How old are you?"

"I'm seven. I just had my birthday."

"Nice! I'm seven and a half. My birthday is in February."

"Cool! Are you new?" Sally asked. "Where are you from?"

"I'm from California," I said.

"Wow, that's really far away!"

I wanted to talk more with Sally, but then class started. Mrs. Potts told us the classroom rules. There were too many rules to remember.

Soon, it was lunchtime. I wanted to sit with Sally, but her table was full, so I had to go sit somewhere else. I found a table that had a few extra seats and sat at the very edge.

Back at my old school, I always sat with Diya and Izzy, my two best friends. With them by my side, I never felt lonely. But now, with no one to call my friend, I felt really alone, like the lost penguin in a nature show I had watched with Dad. The little penguin was all alone, a black speck on the white ice, with its friends and family miles and miles away. I cried when I watched that episode, and I kind of felt like crying now.

I took out my lunch box, which had a golden retriever puppy on it. It always made me happy, because the puppy looked like it was smiling.

Well, I thought. *At least my lunch box is cute.*

I opened it and took out my seaweed, kimchi, rolled eggs, and rice.

"What is that?" asked a girl at my table. She pointed at my dried seaweed packs.

"Dried seaweed!" I said. "It's yummy."

"And that?" She pointed at my kimchi.

I blinked at her. How could she not know what kimchi was?

"It's kimchi," I explained. "It's spicy cabbage."

She wrinkled her nose. "It smells."

"Wait," said a boy sitting next to her. "Did she just say that she was eating *seaweed*? Like, from the ocean?"

He laughed, and a few of his friends joined in too. By then *everyone* at the table was staring at me. My cheeks turned bright red.

Suddenly, I wasn't hungry anymore. I wanted to run far, far away. Or go hide in the bathroom somewhere. But we had to go back to class soon, so it wasn't really worth the trouble.

From across the room, Sally frowned at me but didn't say anything.

I thought at least recess would be fun, but being the new kid was boring. Everyone else, including Sally, already had friends to play with. I ended up sitting on the swings by myself. I have always loved swinging, kicking my legs super fast to see if I can go over the top of the swings. But it's not as fun if you're swinging alone.

I hated being the new kid.

Chapter 4

Finally, my very first day ended. Eunice-unni came to pick me up after school. Dad usually works late, so he hired her as my babysitter. *Unni* means "big sister" in Korean. She's not really my sister, but I have to call her that to be polite. Yeah, it's pretty confusing for me, too.

Eunice-unni is in high school. Dad and I met her over the weekend so we could make sure she was okay. I asked her the important questions like, "Do you think puppies are cute?" and "What is your favorite type of ice cream?"

She agreed that puppies are cute but then said that her favorite ice cream flavor is vanilla.

One out of two is better than nothing, I guess.

Eunice-unni said I could meet her dog when she picked me up from school. I ran when I saw her car in the parking lot. It was easy to find because it was blue.

"I like your car," I said. "Blue is my favorite color."

"It's mine, too!"

That was almost enough to make up for the fact that her favorite ice cream flavor was vanilla. Almost.

"Can I really meet your dog today?"

"Yes!" Eunice-unni beamed so I could see her braces. "You can play with him at my house. He's a little Maltese named Oliver. I'm so excited for you to meet him!"

I was excited to meet Oliver too! I'd only seen pictures of Maltese dogs, and they looked so fluffy! I bounced up and down in my seat.

Eunice-unni drove us to her house. Her mom was there and so was Oliver!

Oliver jumped up and down when I walked into the house. I got down to my knees, and he started licking my face. He was so cute and looked like a soft

little cloud. I wished I had a dog like him. "Maltese" was now officially on the list of my favorite dog breeds.

Mrs. Park, Eunice-unni's mom, came over to say hi. She was wearing plastic gloves covered with red pepper paste. I could tell by the smell coming from the kitchen that she was making kimchi.

"Hi, Mindy, it's so nice to meet you!" said Mrs. Park. "I've heard so many things about you!"

I hate when grown-ups say that. You never know if they've heard good things or bad things. I smiled big and wide, just in case.

"How was school?" Mrs. Park asked.

"School was okay," I said.

I didn't tell them about what happened at lunch. I was still too embarrassed.

"Can I go play with Oliver until my dad comes?" I asked Eunice-unni before Mrs. Park could ask me any more questions.

"Sure! His box of toys is in the living room."

I ran to the living room, with Oliver following close behind. My day was better already.

How could I be sad with a cute dog nearby?

Chapter 5

The next morning, Dad packed me the same thing for lunch: rice, dried seaweed, kimchi, and rolled eggs. I meant to tell him that I wanted something different, but we didn't have time. Our toaster had caught on fire, so Dad was already late for work.

"I didn't know you were supposed to clean the toaster," Dad said as he drove me to school. "Your mom must have always taken care of it before she got sick."

I didn't know that either, but I was surprised Dad didn't. Dad is a grown up. Aren't grown-ups supposed to know everything?

The second day of school was less scary than

the first. But I was still nervous about lunch. What if everyone laughed at me again?

I decided to be a little brave and make goals. Dad says he always has to "make goals" at his job. Things that you want to happen. Goals sounded like something adults made, but I was trying to be more grown-up now.

At my desk, I flipped over to a new page in my Shiba Inu notebook and wrote down my goals in sparkly blue ink.

1. Don't get laughed at during lunch again.
2. Try to make a new friend.
3. Convince Dad that a puppy would be the best idea ever.

It wasn't going to be easy, but I did feel kind of better after writing everything down.

Class passed by really quickly, and soon it was time for lunch. Before Sally left, I took a deep breath and said, "Hey, Sally. Can I sit with you at your lunch table?"

I was scared that she'd say no, but I reminded myself to be a little brave.

Sally looked surprised but smiled. "Okay, sure!"

Phew! I smiled back. That wasn't so bad! And now I had someone who actually wanted to eat lunch with me!

Sally and I walked to her table. But instead of feeling glad that I was sitting with Sally, I still felt super nervous. What if Sally and her friends made fun of my food too?

I slowly opened my lunch box and all my containers. Everyone at the table stared, just like they did yesterday.

I was prepared to be laughed at again when Sally held out her hand. "Can I try some of the seaweed?"

"What?" I asked, surprised.

Sally shrugged. "My mom always says I should try things out before I decide I don't like them."

I handed her the packet of seaweed. It was the spicy kind that you can eat as a snack without rice.

She opened the packet and put a little piece of seaweed in her mouth.

She chewed, her eyes wide.

I was worried that she didn't like it, but then she exclaimed, "Hey! This is really good!"

Everyone looked at Sally. Then, a boy from our class—Charlie, I think— asked, "Can I try too?"

"Sure!"

Charlie ate the seaweed. But the moment it touched his mouth, he spat it back out. "Ew! It feels so weird! Like paper!"

Sally rolled her eyes. "You didn't even eat it!"

"Let me try!" another boy said.

"You better actually eat it, Dill," said Sally. "Don't spit it out like Charlie."

"I won't!"

Sally nodded at me, and I handed Dill a piece of seaweed.

Unlike Charlie, Dill kept the seaweed in his mouth and chewed. "Wow, this is actually good!"

"Well, of course it's good!" I replied. "If you didn't know what dried seaweed was for all this time, you've been missing out!"

Soon everyone at my table was asking to try the dried seaweed. Before I knew it, I didn't have any left for myself.

I ate the rest of my lunch, but it wasn't the same. I was happy that no one had teased me today, but I was sad I didn't have any seaweed left for me. My plan had worked well—too well!

"Sorry everyone ate your seaweed," said Sally. "You should have asked us to trade something with you!"

"I can do that?" I asked.

"Sure, why not? You gave us something. Shouldn't you get something in return? It's only fair."

She had a point. I looked around. Everyone else was still enjoying their lunches. They all had cool snacks too, like Oreos, Pringles, Nutella bites, and fruit snacks. We always just got Korean snacks, because Dad only had time to go shopping at the Korean market. I love Korean snacks, but eating the same snacks over and over again gets kind of boring.

My mouth watered. I was surrounded by these yummy snacks, and all I had for lunch was boring white rice and side dishes. And I still didn't have any friends except maybe Sally.

I kept on thinking as I ate the rest of my sad lunch.

Suddenly, I had a brilliant plan. A very yummy seaweed business plan!

Chapter 6

When Dad picked me up from Eunice-unni's house later that evening, I asked, "Can we stop by the Korean market?"

Dad frowned. "What do you need to buy? We already have a lot of food at home."

"It's for school," I said. "It's important!"

Dad looked confused, but he drove to the Korean market without any more questions. There aren't a lot of Asian markets in Florida, and the closest Korean one is an hour away, in Orlando. And that meant we were super close to Disney World!

When he told me that we were going to move to

Florida, Dad promised to take me to Disney World. I reminded him of the promise.

"I'll take you there when things are less busy at work, sweetie," he said.

I knew it meant that we'd probably never go. It made me sad, but it's not Dad's fault. He's always busy, and he worked really hard when we were back in California too. I just wish his boss gave him more breaks.

The Korean market in Orlando isn't as big as the one in California. It's also really old. But it still has all my favorite snacks, like Pepero chocolate sticks, Choco Pie, and shrimp crackers. So it's okay in my book.

Today, though, I didn't go for any of those snacks. I was on a mission. It was time to put part one of Operation Yummy Seaweed Business in motion!

I ran right for the dried seaweed aisle. Since people like to eat seaweed with all sorts of stuff, there are lots of different kinds of seaweed on the shelves: dried seaweed that you put in soup, salted seaweed that you eat with rice, and large, plain seaweed sheets that you use to wrap kimbap and sushi.

I grabbed a bunch of spicy seaweed snacks and put them in our shopping basket.

Dad raised his eyebrows. "This is for school?" he asked.

I gave him a firm nod. He still looked suspicious but didn't make me put any back.

I dropped a few more packs of different-flavored seaweed snacks into the basket too.

Dad shot me another weird look. "Okay, Mindy, I think you have enough to last you until winter break."

I gave Dad a big smile but didn't say anything.

After a few more minutes of wandering the store, Dad yawned. "Ready to go, kiddo?"

I grabbed his hand and gave him my best smile.

"Yes. Thanks, Appa," I said.

He hugged me. "Sure."

I glanced back toward the snacks. "Wait, can we get some Choco Pies before we leave?"

Dad grinned, like he knew I was going to ask him that. He always knows everything.

He ruffled my hair. "Why not? We need to celebrate your first few days of school anyway."

When we got home, we ate our Choco Pies. That night I dreamed of pies, California, and seaweed, and hoped my third day of school would go just how I wanted.

Chapter 7

On Wednesday morning, I told Dad to put ten packs of the seaweed into my lunch box.

"Ten? You will never eat all of those in one day, Mindy," Dad said.

"It's an experiment!" I replied. "Plus, I want to share with some of the kids in my class."

It wasn't a complete lie. Dad sighed, but he stuffed all ten packs of seaweed into my lunch box. Along with the rice and side dishes, my lunch box looked extra full. I was afraid that it might explode and seaweed would fly out everywhere. But it didn't.

At school, I sat next to Sally again. She had blue ribbons in her hair today, and they reminded me of the ocean. Mom, Dad, and I loved to go to the beach in California. Even though there was one right by my new school, I didn't know when I'd be able to go with Dad.

At lunch, Dill asked, "Do you have any more of that dried seaweed?"

Sally shot me a look, and I crossed my arms. It was my chance!

"Yeah, but you have to trade me something for it!" I said.

He shrugged. "Okay. I have gummy worms. Do you want some?"

He held up a small baggie of sour gummy worms. They were green apple-flavored. My favorite!

"Sure! Let's shake on it."

I held out my hand, like I had seen people do on TV. He shook my hand, and then we swapped snacks.

"Hey," said a girl with red hair. Her nose was wrinkled, but she held out a bag of Cheetos. "I want to try the seaweed everyone is talking about. Want to trade?"

"Sure! What's your name?"

"Amanda."

"Hi, I'm Mindy!"

I shook hands with her, too.

Soon a whole line of people had formed to trade snacks with me. I wasn't sure if I had enough!

"Wow!" Sally said. "It looks like business is booming!"

She said it kind of funny, like she was just repeating something she'd heard on TV.

"Yup, and it's all thanks to you! Thanks for the idea."

"No problem."

She gave me a big grin.

"Hey," I said. "Do you want some of the snacks everyone gave me? I can't eat this all by myself!"

"Sure, thanks!"

I gave Sally half of my pile of snacks. She grinned, and we happily munched on everything for the rest of lunch.

The plan was working!

Chapter 8

The next day, a line of kids formed in the cafeteria even before I got out my packs of seaweed.

"Okay," I said. "Everyone, show me your snacks!"

I examined the snacks to see which ones were the best. Everyone had pretty good snacks, except the kids with vegetable sticks and vanilla cake. Dad always makes me eat vegetables at home, so there was no way I was going to eat them at school. And vanilla is just gross. Plain and simple.

When I skipped over the boy with the vanilla cake, he said, "Hey! How come everyone else gets to trade with you except me?"

"I don't like vanilla, sorry," I said. I wasn't really

sorry, but Dad always says it's polite to apologize when someone is upset. And this boy looked *really* mad! His face was turning red like a tomato. He looked like he was going to cry.

I almost told him that he could get the seaweed packs himself at the Korean market. But I didn't. Because then everyone would hear, and no one would need me to trade snacks with them any-more. I'd have no friends left.

I decided to ignore him. Maybe he'd just go back to his seat.

But instead of leaving, the boy stood there, staring angrily at me and the other kids as I traded snacks with them.

Sally came over to sit next to me.

"That's Brandon," she whispered. "Don't worry about him. He's a big baby. No one really likes him."

She glared at Brandon until he finally walked back to his table.

"Thanks," I said.

"No problem!"

At recess, Sally and I were on the swings together when she asked, "Did you ever think about *selling* the seaweed snacks?"

I almost fell off my swing. "Huh?"

"I mean, think about it! Everyone loves the snacks a *lot*. And getting snacks back for them is good, but then you have to eat everything and it's too much food. What if you ask for money instead?"

"But what would I do with the money? I don't need to buy anything."

Sally shrugged. "It was just a suggestion. My mom says you have to take advantage of every good business opportunity. She works for a really big company and is always saying that."

"Wow, that's so cool!"

Sally talking about her mom made me miss my mom. I wished my mom were here to give me good advice too.

I got off my swing. There were only a few minutes left of recess.

"Tag, you're it!" I tapped Sally on the shoulder before breaking into a run.

"Hey, I wasn't ready!" Sally protested, but she jumped off her swing and started chasing me anyway.

She caught me right away, but I wasn't mad.

Did I finally have my first real friend at school?

Chapter 9

Dad was working late today, so Eunice-unni came over to our house to stay with me. The house was big and scary without Dad, but Eunice-unni brought Oliver the Maltese with her, so it was okay!

I played fetch with Oliver while Eunice-unni finished her homework. Oliver was so fluffy that whenever he ran, he looked like a bouncing cloud. He was *so* cute.

Seeing Oliver run around our house made me want a dog even more. Playing with him made me so happy!

"Hey, Mindy," said Eunice-unni. "I'm done with

my homework. Wanna walk Oliver around the block with me?"

"Sure!"

Eunice-unni let me hold Oliver's leash as we walked around my neighborhood. Compared to my old neighborhood, everything was so *green*. There were palm trees and bushes everywhere, like in a jungle. My neighbors all had really big yards with tall grass. Back in California, it didn't rain much, so everything was brown. Florida seemed like a whole different planet!

Oliver got really muddy from wandering outside. Eunice-unni said it was okay, since we could just wash him in the bathtub.

"He needed a bath anyway," she said with a smile.

Dad didn't get home until really late. By the time the garage door opened, Eunice-unni and I had already finished bathing Oliver and eaten dinner.

When he got home, Dad was so tired that he fell asleep on the couch!

I nudged him softly on the shoulder.

"Appa," I said. "Shouldn't you sleep in your bed?"

Dad startled awake, but then relaxed when he saw me.

"Oh, hi, Mindy," he said, rubbing his eyes. "Yeah, I really should. What time is it?"

"It's ten. Can you tuck me into bed?"

"Oh wow. And I haven't eaten dinner yet."

I gasped. "You didn't eat dinner at work?"

"No, I didn't have time. It's fine. I'll grab something later. Come on, sweetie. Let's go."

Dad tucked me in, but I couldn't sleep because I was too worried. Dad was so tired! And he forgot to eat dinner! What if he got sick like Mom?

I decided to take matters into my own hands. I'm not sure exactly what that means, but I've heard Dad say it before. I think it means doing things yourself.

After Dad finished eating and went to his room, I got out of bed and tiptoed to the kitchen. I'm not allowed to touch the stove yet, but Dad says I can use the electric kettle to boil water since all you have to do is press the switch. I put water in the kettle and turned it on.

As the water started to boil, I got on my step

stool so I could reach the tea. Dad bought a cute pink step stool with white hearts just for me! With the stool, I could reach for a chamomile tea bag with no problem. Dad likes to drink chamomile tea because he says it helps him relax. I couldn't wait to surprise him with the tea!

I carefully carried the mug of tea to Dad's room. I was about to open the bedroom door when I heard sniffling noises. Dad was crying!

"Appa!"

With one hand still clutching the mug, I flung open the door.

"Mindy!" Dad bolted up from the bed, like I'd caught him doing something wrong. He looked really embarrassed!

But he was also definitely crying. Ever since Mom died, Dad cries all the time.

"I made you some tea so you could feel better!" I held out the cup of tea.

Dad smiled, but he still looked sad. "Thank you, Mindy. That's really sweet of you. Now please go back to bed. It's way past your bedtime."

"Okay. Good night, Dad."

"Good night." He took a sip of the tea and waved.

I went back to my room. But even when I was in my bed, I kept thinking about how sad Dad looked. And then I thought about how I always felt better whenever I played with Oliver.

I wanted to cheer up Dad, but I couldn't do it alone. Maybe Sally was right. Maybe I could sell my seaweed snacks for money. Then, I could buy a puppy for Dad and me! Since it's impossible to be sad with a cute puppy around, Dad wouldn't be so sad and lonely, and I could have the dog I'd always wanted. It'd be like hitting two birds with one stone!

I snuck downstairs, got Dad's tablet, and brought it back to my room. Puppies are expensive if you buy them from breeders, but not if you adopt them from a shelter!

On the Internet, I found a nearby shelter and scrolled through the available dogs. They were all so cute that I couldn't choose! But they also looked so sad, kind of like Dad.

Don't worry! I thought while scrolling through

the dog pictures. *I'll adopt one of you guys soon!*
Then you and Dad can both be happy.

After a while, I started getting sleepy. I set Dad's
tablet down next to me on the bed and fell asleep,
dreaming of cute puppies and Dad's smiling face.

Chapter 10

On Friday, Dad didn't say anything when I packed dozens of seaweed snacks into my bag. He didn't say anything at all. I think he was too tired. And sad.

Don't worry, Dad! I thought. *I'll get us a puppy real soon!*

During quiet reading time, I went to the back of the classroom. Mrs. Potts looked up from where she was grading worksheets.

"Mindy?" she said with a frown. "Is everything all right?"

"Yup!" I gave her a big smile. "I finished my book, so I just wanted to get markers and paper so I could draw, if that's okay!"

"Well, all right."

She went back to her work, and I got out my box of markers and a piece of paper from my desk.

"I'm gonna do it!" I whispered to Sally. "Operation Yummy Seaweed Business is a go!"

Sally whispered back, "That's great! What are the markers and paper for?"

"You'll see!"

On the paper, I wrote in big letters: SEAWEED SNACKS FOR SALE. ONLY $1 EACH!

I put a smiley face at the bottom of the paper as a finishing touch.

"Nice!" Sally said. "It'll get people's attention for sure!"

When it was lunchtime, I opened my lunch box to show everyone my seaweed snacks. Beside me, Sally held up the sign I made.

"Attention!" I said to the table. "From now on, you can get a seaweed snack for only one dollar each! This is a good deal! Candy from the cafeteria costs *at least* two dollars."

Everyone seemed to think a dollar was a good

price. At least, no one complained. Like they had the day before, everyone lined up for a seaweed snack. I didn't have anywhere to put the dollar bills, so I ended up putting all of them in my lunch box.

And Sally was right: business was booming!

Lunch was almost over when Brandon came over to my table. He grinned at me, but not in a nice way.

"You know it's against the rules to sell things at school, right?"

I looked at Sally with wide eyes. She stared back at me. I don't think she knew that rule either.

"You're making it up!" Sally said, crossing her arms in front of her chest.

Brandon stuck his nose in the air. "No, I'm not. I'm telling on you two."

He glanced around from left to right. I didn't have to be a mind reader to know that he was looking for a teacher. Brandon broke into a run.

"Stop him!" I yelled at Sally.

Sally chased after Brandon. I wanted to chase

Brandon right away too, but I had to make sure the money was safely in my lunch box first.

We ran as fast as we could across the cafeteria. But it was too late. Before Sally or I could catch him, Brandon ran to Mrs. Potts, who was on lunch duty today.

Brandon took a big breath.

"No!" Sally and I both screamed.

Mrs. Potts looked at us, confused. "Is everything all right, girls?"

Brandon yelled, "Mrs. Potts! Mindy is selling her seaweed snacks! That's against the rules!"

Everyone sitting at the tables around us froze. I gulped. Sally looked pretty scared too.

Mrs. Potts looked more confused than angry. "Selling her . . . seaweed snacks? What do you mean, Brandon?"

"Mindy is selling her weird seaweed snacks for money," whined Brandon. "She has dollar bills crammed in her lunch box."

Mrs. Potts turned to look at me. "Is this true, Mindy?"

I stared down at my feet. My lips started trembling. All I wanted was to make Dad happy. I didn't know selling my snacks would get me in trouble.

"Mindy?" Mrs. Potts tried again. "Can you please look up at me?"

I did. Mrs. Potts was frowning at me like she had on the first day of school, when she couldn't say my Korean name. Everyone else was staring at me too. Even Sally.

Suddenly, I was really mad. Why was I the only one getting in trouble, when asking for money wasn't even *my* idea in the first place?

I pointed at Sally. "It was *her* idea!" I blurted. "I was trading snacks when Sally told me I should ask for money. I didn't even know it was against the rules! No one told me. I just moved here!"

It worked. Mrs. Potts looked at Sally, surprised. "Sally? Is this true?"

Sally's mouth dropped open. Her eyes got really shiny all of a sudden, like she was about to cry. I felt really bad.

"I never *told* you that you should!" Sally yelled

at me. "I only suggested it. You didn't *have* to ask for money."

"You two are both bad!" Brandon interrupted. "You need to get kicked out of school!"

"What are you even talking about?" Sally yelled at him. "Shut up!"

"Yeah, Brandon. Be quiet! Why would we get kicked out of school?"

"Everyone, please!" Mrs. Potts yelled, stopping all of us.

By then, a big crowd had formed around us to see all the action.

"Take deep breaths to calm down. Brandon, no one is getting kicked out of school, and you are in trouble too, for running around the cafeteria and causing a commotion."

I cheered on the inside.

"All three of you, walk down to the principal's office right now. I'll have to call your parents."

"What?" Sally yelled. "Thanks a lot, Mindy."

"Why are you blaming me for *your* idea?"

"Miss Johnson! Miss Kim! Please go to the principal's office at once!"

Oh boy. Mrs. Potts used the last name card. I was *really* in trouble now.

I sighed and walked out of the cafeteria with Sally and Brandon.

Chapter 11

Even before he spoke, I knew that our principal was gonna be really mean and scary, and not just because his name is Dr. Mortimer. He is really skinny and tall, and behind his square glasses, he has big, bulging eyes like a bat. Only, bats are pretty cute once you get over the fact that they look like little aliens. Dr. Mortimer isn't cute at all.

He looked up from his computer when I came in. I really wished the secretary had let me come in with Sally or even with Brandon—*that* was how much I didn't want to be in Dr. Mortimer's office alone. I'd figured we would all be getting in trouble together. But no such luck. She'd said the principal would see us one by one.

"Min-jung Kim?" he asked, peering down at me over his narrow glasses. His voice was all gravelly, like it belonged to a monster in a scary movie. I'm not supposed to watch scary movies, but once, I snuck downstairs to watch one while Dad was asleep. Afterward, I was so scared that I had to sleep with my night-light on for two whole months.

"That's me," I said, sitting in front of his desk. "But I go by Mindy."

"Mindy . . . ," he said. But unlike Mrs. Potts, Dr. Mortimer didn't seem happy with my nickname. "So, Mrs. Potts told me that you were selling snacks on school property. Is that true?"

Dad always said it was good to be honest, so I replied, "Yes, but I didn't know it was against the school rules. I just moved here this week!"

"I see." Dr. Mortimer frowned. He looked at his computer screen again. "And what is this about . . . seaweed?"

He sounded really confused.

"My dad always packs me seaweed snacks from the Korean market. Everyone really liked them, so I traded with everybody for their snacks before I started asking for money."

"Seaweed snacks?" He wrinkled his nose.

"They're yummy! I have some if you want to try—"

"That won't be necessary," Dr. Mortimer said, cutting me off.

He looked at me like my grandma looks at flies while trying to catch them with a swatter. "Selling snacks is strictly forbidden on school grounds. I will let you off with a warning this time because you are new, but please familiarize yourself with the school rules during the weekend before returning to school on Monday. They're online, so you can get your parents to show them to you. Please return to class, Miss Kim. I will e-mail your teacher to let her know my decision."

I didn't even get the chance to tell Dr. Mortimer that I only have one parent, not two. He turned back toward his computer right away. The conversation was over. And so was my seaweed business.

Chapter 12

For the rest of the day, Sally ignored me. She didn't look at me one bit, even though our seats were right next to each other.

Mrs. Potts called all our parents, and I heard someone say that Sally cried in the bathroom while Mrs. Potts called her mom. Mrs. Potts also tried calling my dad, but she had to leave a message. I hoped Dad would forget to call her back.

Even though Sally *had* been the one to tell me that I could sell my seaweed snacks, I still felt kind of bad about getting her into trouble too. She was the first and only friend I'd made here at Wishbone Elementary, but I wasn't sure if we were friends anymore. I'd have no one to play with on the playground again.

Back at home, Dad asked, "How was school today?"

Eunice-unni's mom had given us kimchi dumplings when Dad picked me up, and he was heating them in a pan on the stove as he talked to me. Even though I like dumplings, I wasn't sure if Dad was cooking them right. There was too much hot oil splattering loudly everywhere, the drops all dancing in the pan a little too fast.

"It was . . . okay," I said.

"Just okay?"

Dad's voice sounded weird, a little higher than usual. I hoped against hope that he hadn't heard Mrs. Potts's message.

CRACKLE-CRACKLE-POP! Suddenly, some of the oil splattered out of the pan and onto Dad.

"Ouch!" He jumped back.

"Appa!" I yelled. "Are you okay?"

When Dad turned to look at me, there were tears in his eyes, but he was still smiling. He does that a lot. I think it's because he doesn't want me to worry.

"I'm fine, sweetie. Nothing that good ol' cold water won't fix."

He turned off the stove and turned on the kitchen sink so he could stick his hand into the water.

Then, Dad cleared his throat and asked, "So, what's this about the principal's office? I got a call from Mrs. Potts earlier, but I was waiting for you to bring it up first."

There it was. I sighed.

"I was trading snacks with the other kids," I began. The more I talked, the more my words came tumbling out in a rush. "But then my friend Sally and I got the idea to sell the snacks for money. I didn't know selling snacks was against the rules, but it is, and someone told on us. So we got sent to the principal's office."

"Selling snacks? What snacks?" Dad looked really confused.

"Seaweed snacks," I said.

"Oh. So *that's* why you needed to pack so many seaweed snacks. You know, you can always ask me if you need something, Mindy. I don't understand why you felt the need to sell snacks to raise money. I hope you returned all the money you got from the kids. What did you even need the money for?"

"Mrs. Potts and the other teachers returned the money to everyone," I said. "And . . . I wanted it to be a surprise."

Dad frowned. "A surprise?"

I nodded sadly. "I know you're still sad because Mom died, so I wanted to cheer you up by buying you a puppy. Because puppies make me happy, and I want you to be happy too."

Suddenly, Dad looked like he was about to cry again. "Oh, Mindy. You didn't have to do that."

He pulled me into a big hug.

There were some sniffly sounds, but when Dad finally pulled away, he quickly wiped away his tears. He looked really embarrassed.

"You don't have to be embarrassed, Dad. You can cry. Everyone gets sad sometimes."

Mom used to always tell me that when I cried. Dad must have recognized the words, because his eyes started watering again.

"I know, Mindy. But I can't help but think that this wouldn't have happened if I were a little better at being a dad. I'm so sorry, Mindy."

"No!" I yelled. "You are the best dad. You do everything you can to make me happy. You're just really busy, that's all."

Dad sighed. "I know. I have to fix that."

After he finished making the dumplings, Dad asked, "So . . . why did you feel the need to trade snacks in the first place? Mindy, if you're not happy with the snacks I pack you, you can always tell me."

I shook my head. "It wasn't because of the snacks. Well, okay. At first, it was because everyone else had really cool snacks. But then, I did it to make friends. Everyone liked me when I gave them seaweed snacks. They talked to me too."

"Aw, you don't need snacks to make people like you, Mindy! I'm sure people will love you just the way you are, like they did in California."

I shook my head again. "No, they won't. It's not the same. I'm the only Asian girl in the entire school! Everyone made fun of me on the first day. Now, some kids still look at me kind of funny, but they all talked to me when we traded snacks."

"I'm sorry, sweetie. The snack thing was a good idea, but try to find another way to make friends, okay? One that won't get you into trouble. I know it's hard, but I have complete faith in you, Mindy. You're a smart girl, and I'm sure you'll figure something out."

I sighed.

"Okay," I said, even though I had no idea how I was gonna make new friends. "I'll try."

Chapter 13

On Monday morning, I didn't want to go to school. I didn't even want to get out of bed!

I pulled my blanket over my head. Maybe if I hid well enough, Dad would forget I was here and leave the house without me.

I'd promised Dad that I would try to make new friends again, but I was still scared. Without my snack-trading business, no one would want to talk to me. Sally was still mad at me. And I didn't want to be alone.

Soft footsteps came from the staircase. Then, Dad was there, sitting on the edge of my bed. He

gently pulled the covers down, and I gave him my
best sad-puppy-dog face.

"Appa, do I *have* to go to school?"

He smiled. "Yup, it's a Monday. That
means school for you and work for me.
Mindy, why don't you ask a friend if she

wants to come over during the weekend? That way you'll have something to look forward to and the week will fly right by."

I sighed. "But I don't have anyone to play with."

Dad frowned. "Didn't you say you had a friend from school? Her name was Sally, right?"

I picked at my blanket. "Sally isn't my friend anymore. We had a fight because she was the one who said I should sell seaweed snacks in the first place."

Dad frowned. "Oh, Mindy. I'm sure she only meant to help. Why don't you apologize and invite her over to our house?"

I pulled the covers over my head again. "What if she says no?"

Instead of answering, Dad slowly placed his hands on my sides and started wiggling his fingers up and down. He was tickling me!

"Ah!" I yelled, bursting out of my blankets. "That tickles!"

Dad let go, and I leaped out of bed.

"Always works like a charm." Dad chuckled.

"Come on, Mindy. You're going to be late for school, and I'm going to be late for work."

I didn't care about being late for school. But I didn't want Dad to be late for work.

"Okay," I said sadly.

To make myself feel better, I dragged myself out of bed and went to my closet. I picked out a corgi T-shirt and bright pink pants. Cute clothes always make me feel a tiny bit better, even on days I feel gloomy.

Dad smiled when he saw my outfit.

"Very cute! Let's go."

I put on my pink Crocs and got into the car.

Chapter 14

Mrs. Potts announced that the whole class was banned from trading snacks. "Banned," she explained, meant that we weren't allowed to do something. Trading snacks technically wasn't against school rules, but she didn't want us to get any other ideas.

Everyone looked disappointed, but no one looked as disappointed as I was.

Now that we weren't allowed to trade snacks anymore, no one even glanced my way. Sally was still ignoring me. It was like I was a ghost.

I was kind of mad at Sally. If it weren't for her, I'd have been able to keep my snack trading ring and would still have friends. Why was *she* still mad at me for something *she* did?

But then I thought about what Dad had said about Sally just trying to help. That was probably true. She *was* trying to be helpful.

When it was time for lunch, Sally left the classroom without me, so I ate alone. It made me so sad that I made up my mind. I was going to say sorry to Sally during recess. Or try to, anyway.

When the bell rang for recess, I slowly walked outside. There was no point in running to the playground like everyone else. I had no one to play with. It was really sunny, and there wasn't a cloud in the sky. I could hear seagulls crying above my head.

I stared up at the seagulls. If only the birds could be my friends.

When I got to the swings, I saw Sally playing with a few other girls. The girls waved at me, but Sally turned her head and pretended not to see me.

I looked down at my Crocs. They're pink and have little Shiba Inu puppy pins on them. The Crocs are my favorite pair of shoes, since they're the last shoes Mom bought for me.

Mom always said I should try my best to be nice to other kids. And so did Dad.

I decided I needed to try my best right then and there. I scrunched up my hands into fists and said in a loud voice, "Sally, I'm sorry!"

Everyone went quiet. I looked up to see that everyone around us was staring at Sally and me. But I didn't care. I was here on a mission.

Sally still had her back turned toward me. Her shoulders were tensed up, so I knew she wasn't ready to forgive me yet. But at least she was listening.

I continued, "I know you were just trying to help when you said I should sell my seaweed snacks. You're right. I didn't *have* to follow your suggestion. I'm sorry I got you into trouble too. Can we still be friends?"

Sally slowly turned around. She didn't look like she completely forgave me, but it was a start.

"Thanks for saying sorry. My mom was mad at me, and I got yelled at a lot."

I felt bad. I wished there were a way to make it up to Sally.

"I'm really sorry," I said. "Do you want me to push you on the swings? I'll push you if you push me next."

She shrugged. "Okay."

I ran to the swings. Sally sat down, and I pushed her so she went flying into the air.

"WHEE!" she yelled.

She looked happy, and I was happy that she was happy. Her ponytail bounced up and down as she rode the swings.

Then, it was my turn. Sally got off, and I sat down. The seat was warm from Sally's butt.

Sally pushed me so I went up, up into the sky. From way up high, I could see the ocean! The water was blue and super pretty, and so was the white sand on the beach next to our school. I wished we were allowed to go there during recess.

Too soon, we had to go back to class. And for the first time, I was sad to leave the playground.

Chapter 15

During our class visit to the school library, I was reading a book about sleepovers when I remembered what Dad had said about inviting Sally over. Hopefully, a sleepover could help patch things up between Sally and me for good.

"Hey," I whispered to Sally. "Wanna sleep over at my house on Friday? We have lots of good snacks, not just seaweed! You can have all the snacks you want."

I was afraid she'd say no, but Sally said, "Sounds fun! I'll ask my mom, and she'll call your mom. What's your number?"

I froze, like I always do when someone mentions Mom.

Sally looked worried. "What's wrong?"

I didn't want Sally to know I didn't have a mom. Not yet. Back in my old school, kids always looked at me funny after they found out what happened to my mom.

"I live with my dad," I finally said. "She can call him!"

Sally shrugged. "Okay!"

And I was pretty happy for the rest of the day. Even though I didn't have my seaweed business, maybe my plan had worked a little after all. I actually felt like I had a new friend. Maybe this school wouldn't be as bad as I thought.

After school, Eunice-unni and I drove back to my house. Dad said he was working late today again, so we were prepared with a whole list of games.

But when we got home, I saw Dad's car parked in the driveway.

"That's weird," said Eunice-unni. "Did I miss a text from him or something? I could have sworn he said he was gonna be late today."

She walked me to the door and rang the bell. Dad opened the door, grinning wide.

"Hi, Eunice. Sorry I didn't give you the heads-up. I was able to reschedule some things today, so I decided to come home early to spend more time with Mindy. Thanks for dropping her off!"

Eunice-unni smiled. She looked happy that I could spend more time with Dad.

"No problem," she said. "Have fun, Mindy!"

Dad and I waved as she left.

"Okay, Mindy. I have a surprise for you. Close your eyes and take my hand."

It was a weird thing for Dad to ask, but I closed my eyes and grabbed his hand anyway. I trusted him!

Gently, Dad pulled me forward. As we moved, I tried to picture where we were in the house. And I wondered what was going on.

"Okay, open your eyes," Dad said at last.

At first, I was confused. Even though I had

opened my eyes, everything was still dark!

But then I saw them. Five small candles. And below the candles was . . .

"A MINT CHOCOLATE CHIP ICE CREAM CAKE!" I shrieked. "But it's not even my birthday!"

Dad turned the lights back on. He stood there by the table with a grin on his face.

"I know," he said. "But I wanted to congratulate you on making it through your first week at your new school! I was actually planning something for last Friday, but the timing was bad since that's when you got in trouble. So we're celebrating today!"

"Thanks, Dad." I gave him a big hug. "Does this mean I can get a puppy for my birthday?"

Dad looked confused. "Huh?"

"Well, you can't do the surprise candles and ice cream cake again since you already did it now. Doing the same thing twice is boring. The only way to make things *even better* for my birthday is to get me a puppy!"

Dad laughed. "You are a tough customer, Mindy.

Let's settle in a little longer, and we'll see. We can save up some money for one."

It wasn't a yes, but it was better than a no. I still had a chance at the puppy!

Dad cut the ice cream cake into slices and put them onto plates. Two big ones for him and two little ones for me. I ate my ice cream cake so quickly that I almost got a brain freeze.

"Careful!" Dad laughed, his mouth full of ice cream cake. But then he winced. "Ow, brain freeze."

I giggled. "You're so silly, Appa!"

He laughed with me, and soon we were both laughing really loudly.

Maybe things would be okay after all.

Acknowledgments

This book wouldn't have been possible without my life experiences and the many different people I encountered. I moved around a lot as a kid, and at one point, like Mindy, I even moved from California to Florida. I was always "the new kid" and probably wouldn't have made it this far without all the friends I met along the way.

First and foremost, I'd like to thank my parents, who tried their best to raise me in a country that was entirely new to them. Thank you for giving me the varied experiences that would be so vital to my books. 사랑해요.

Second, I would like to thank the teachers I

had while growing up. Not all of my teachers were good, but most of them were amazing and inspired me in so many different ways. Special thanks goes to Ms. Opal Brown, without whom fourth-grade me would have never even written her first book. Thank you also to Ms. Sheila Holsinger, Ms. Ellen Johnston, and Ms. Silvera. I'd also like to include Janet Ohanis in this category, even though she was already retired by the time I met her. Thank you all for dedicating your lives to teaching kids like me and changing countless lives through your wisdom and encouragement.

A writer is a lost, lonely penguin stranded in the middle of Antarctica without her friends, and I'm so glad I didn't have to go on this journey alone. Thank you to Jennifer Cheung, Allyson Smith, Jason Terry, and the other friends I made nearly twenty years ago at Wadsworth Elementary. We had our differences in the very beginning, but overall, thanks to you, my real-life experience as the new girl in Florida was much happier than Mindy's. Thank you also to my friends from different parts of the country: Chelsea Chang, Shiyun Sun, Luke Chou, Bernice Yau, Anita Chen, Brianna Lei, Annie Lee, Kaiti Liu, and Angelica Tran.

I need a whole other section for my writer friends, because you've all helped me in so many different ways. Thank you to Aneeqah Naeem, my number one cheerleader and "unofficial publicist." Our writing dates were literally life changing, and I hope there are many more to come. Thank you also to Francesca Flores, Akemi Dawn Bowman, Katie Zhao, Amelie Zhao, Rebecca Kuang, Suzie Chang, Elly Ha, Andrea Tang, Dahlia Adler, Marieke Nijkamp, Kat Cho, Axie Oh, Nafiza Azad, and the entirety of the #magicsprintingsquad. I love all of you and wish you the best.

Thank you to my courageous and savvy agent, Penny Moore, and my insightful, fellow-lover-of-cute-things editor, Alyson Heller. You both worked tirelessly to bring Mindy into this world, and I appreciate everything you do. You are basically her honorary aunties. Here's to many more happy tears as we continue on this journey together.

Last but not least, thank you to Andrew Su, who believed in me when I didn't believe in myself. Thanks for the countless times you screamed, "OMG SO CUTE!" whenever I sent you excerpts of Mindy's story. I'm not sure I'd have ever gotten the courage to write this book—and made it as cute as I possibly could—without you.

Don't miss Mindy's next adventure!

My name is Mindy Kim.

I'm almost eight years old, or at least, that's how old I am in the United States. In Korea, though, I'm nine! That's what Dad told me as he drove me to school.

"Korean people calculate age differently," he said. "You're already one year old when you're born, and then you get one year older on New Year's Day, instead of getting older on your birthday."

I got really excited, since it's been eight years since I was born. One plus eight is nine, and nine years old was *definitely* old enough to get a puppy. And even better yet, Lunar New Year was this Saturday!

"Does this mean that I'll turn ten this weekend?" I asked, throwing my backpack in the back seat.

Dad laughed. "No, silly. People only age up on the first of January *or* on Lunar New Year, not both."

I sat back into my seat with a big huff. "What's the point of two New Years if you can only age up on one?"

Dad shook his head as he pulled into the school's parking lot. "It's an important part of our culture, Mindy. It goes way back to the times when our ancestors in Korea used the lunar calendar to tell time. Tell you what, why don't we go to the Lunar New Year parade in Orlando this weekend? I saw an ad for it the other day. It looks like it'll be fun!"

Dad smiled at me, but I was unconvinced. The last time Dad said something would be "fun," I ended up watching a boring show about really slow slugs all by myself because he fell asleep in five minutes.

Plus, so much has changed since the last time we celebrated Lunar New Year. Last year, Dad, Mom, and I celebrated with the other Korean people in our neighborhood. We played really fun games like yutnori and jegichagi, ate so many yummy rice cakes, and even sang karaoke! There was no way that we could have as much fun this year as we did then.

Not without Mom.

Now the only other Korean family in our neighborhood is Eunice's, and they were going to Seattle to visit their relatives for the holiday. It was just going to be me and Dad.

"The parade will be fun," Dad said again. "It'll be good for us to leave the house."

I sighed. Dad really wanted to go to the parade! And I didn't want to make him sad by saying I didn't want to go.

"Okay," I said. "I'll go to the parade."

Dad beamed. "Great! See you after school, honey."

"Bye, Appa," I said, using the Korean word for "Daddy."

I headed toward the school, my shoulders slumped. I was not looking forward to Lunar New Year. Not anymore.

Looking for another great book?
Find it
IN THE MIDDLE.

Fun, fantastic books for kids
in the in-be**TWEEN** age.

IntheMiddleBooks.com

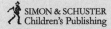 SIMON & SCHUSTER
Children's Publishing   **f** /SimonKids   🐦 @SimonKids

Solve each problem with the smartest third-grade inventor!

EBOOK EDITIONS ALSO AVAILABLE

Aladdin
simonandschuster.com/kids